Also by Joy McCullough

A Field Guide to Getting Lost
Across the Pond

NOT STARRING
Zadie Louise

Joy McCullough

A
atheneum Atheneum Books for Young Readers
New York   London   Toronto   Sydney   New Delhi

ATHENEUM BOOKS FOR YOUNG READERS
An imprint of Simon & Schuster Children's Publishing Division
1230 Avenue of the Americas, New York, New York 10020

For information about special discounts for bulk purchases, please contact Simon & Schuster Special Sales at 1-866-506-1949 or business@simonandschuster.com.
The Simon & Schuster Speakers Bureau can bring authors to your live event. For more information or to book an event, contact the Simon & Schuster Speakers Bureau at 1-866-248-3049 or visit our website at www.simonspeakers.com.
Interior design by Jacquelynne Hudson
The text for this book was set in Excelsior.
Manufactured in the United States of America
0522 FFG
First Edition
10 9 8 7 6 5 4 3 2 1
Library of Congress Cataloging-in-Publication Data
Names: McCullough, Joy, author.
Title: Not starring Zadie Louise / Joy McCullough.
Description: First edition. | New York : Atheneum Books for Young Readers, 2022. | Audience: Ages 8 up. | Summary: With her mom's job and theater on the line, Zadie is determined to help make their show, *Spinderella*, the hit of the season—that is, unless she accidentally turns it into a disaster.
Identifiers: LCCN 2021045837 | ISBN 9781534496231 (hardcover) | ISBN 9781534496255 (ebook)
Subjects: CYAC: Theater—Fiction.
Classification: LCC PZ7.1.M43412 No 2022 | DDC [Fic]—dc23
LC record available at https://lccn.loc.gov/2021045837

For Amy Poisson,
who has a way of dragging me
into the spotlight

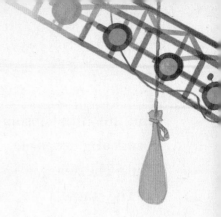

1
No Gravity

These are the most cosmically awesome places at my mom's theater:

The lighting grid, where I pretend I'm an alien, studying the bizarre behavior of the earthlings below. (And I tell you what: actors might as well be a whole other species.)

The trapdoor, but really the hidden space underneath the trapdoor, where it sounds like a rocket ship heading into orbit when a bunch of kids clomp across the stage up above.

The stage manager's booth, with more screens and switches than the control panel at the International Space Station, where I've never been but will go someday.

·····

And this is the absolute-no-doubt-about-it least cosmically awesome place in the Bainbridge Youth Theater:

The stage.

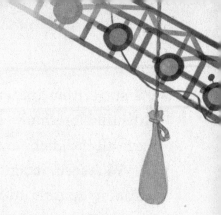

No Special Considerations

"I'm asking you to consider it, Zadie," Mom says as she serves me way too much lasagna. I don't know how she expects me to eat that much, and it's not because I ate a mega pack of Chocoballs right before dinner. "If you're not in the cast, what will you do during all that rehearsal time?"

This will not be a problem.

I will leap from grid to grid, high above the stage, taking extra-special care not to bump the lights. I will hide away underneath the stage, eating way more Chocoballs than Mom would allow if I were in the cast, especially since there is No Food Allowed in the Theater. I will peer down on the stage from the dark booth, pretending I'm Valentina Tereshkova in her rocket while I (don't) move all the knobs and switches.

"You're so imaginative," she says with an alarming sparkle in her eye. "I honestly think you'd make a terrific actor!"

Sometimes my mother makes zero sense. Believing in the possibility of what else is out there beyond our own atmosphere is not at all the same as pretending to be someone else.

Sir Andrew Lloyd Webber weaves in and out of the legs of my chair, mrowling like he agrees with me. I reach down to pick him up but stop when Mom clears her throat in a way that sounds like maybe she has some phlegm, but really, because I'm her daughter, I know means that I am not supposed to pick the cat up when we are sitting at the dinner table.

If I'd gotten to name him, he'd be something awesome, like Yuri Gagarin, first man in space. I didn't get to name him.

"I'm imaginative at Science Kidz," I point out, dropping a little chunk of meat to Sir Andrew Lloyd Webber, even if he has a dumb name. "I imagine what's out there. Whole other life forms! Solar systems!"

"Exactly!" Mom waves the serving spoon and sends a splatter of sauce flying across the room. Papa shakes his head as he goes to retrieve his super-famous secret-formula stain remover. (Okay, it's maybe only famous in our house, and it's not so much a secret as I don't know how he makes it. But he totally makes it. And it works!) "And you could use that imagination at the theater. Other kids practice their auditions for months to get cast in one of my shows. I'm offering you a guaranteed spot."

"It's so unfair," my sister, Lulu, says, clearing her plate and starting on the dishes while the rest of us are still sitting there. "You're always telling me there's no guarantee I'll be cast." Then Lulu puts on her best Mom-face and says in a perfect Mom-voice, "No special considerations."

It's true. Last week Mom gave Lulu a big pep talk about how she didn't need to start wearing vampire eye makeup and ripped jeans just because some other kids her age do. Why does Lulu get to be original, while I'm supposed to do what all the other kids are doing at Bainbridge Youth Theater?

Mom sighs. "You'll definitely be cast in this show. You both will."

"For real?" Lulu stops doing the dishes, then narrows her eyes at Mom. "Why this show?"

Papa comes back in the room with the stain remover. By now Sir Andrew Lloyd Webber is lapping up the sauce that has dribbled down the wall. Instead of going to work on the splattered curtains, Papa sits back down at the table. "Listen, girls," he says. "Things are going to be a little different this summer." He and Mom exchange a glance. One of those grown-up glances where you know they've talked about Whatever It Is when you weren't around, and they've decided Things, and now they're about to tell you How It Is.

"Different how?" Lulu asks, her excitement deflating as she sinks back into her chair.

"Well . . . ," they say together, and then they both blurt out this fake-nervous laugh and say nothing.

"You guys are weirding me out," Lulu says.

I do not like admitting this, but I agree with Lulu.

They try again. This time Mom says, "It's just that—" while at the same time Papa says, "The thing is—" And then they bark-laugh again.

Lulu grabs a roll from the bread basket and shoves it at Papa. "You have the conch," she says.

I have no idea what that means, but Mom sits back with her lips zipped, and Papa nods. Note to self: learn the secret of the dinner roll.

"All right, girls," Papa says, cradling the dinner roll in both hands. "This is a matter that affects the whole family, and you know your mother and I always try to be honest with you."

They're getting divorced! Grandma's dying! An asteroid is hurtling toward the earth as we sit here communing with carbohydrates! I whip my head to look at Mom, but she's far too calm for any of these things to be true.

"Zadie," Papa says. "Don't worry. Just listen. You know that since the academy cut the arts budget, I've been getting by giving private music lessons."

How could I forget? Sometimes he travels to

his students' houses, but for piano they come here. Someone is pounding on those keys pretty much all the time, and not all of them are qualified to command the ship, if you get what I'm saying.

"But it's been a little tight lately. A few of my regular students have gone off to college—"

"Aubrey Benson got into Juilliard!" I cheer.

Papa smiles, but Mom says, "Don't interrupt," and points at the magical bread.

"I'm very proud of Aubrey," Papa says. "But we're just finding we need a bit more income. So I'm going to start driving for Ryde."

"The gig economy," Lulu mutters, shaking her head wearily. Nobody tells her not to interrupt.

"Wait, like a taxi?"

"Basically," he says. "Except I can use my own car, and it's flexible. So I can prioritize music lessons, but drive shifts when it works for my schedule."

"Do that many people use Ryde on the island?" Lulu asks. I wouldn't have thought of that, but everyone I know on the island has their own car.

"Yeah, actually, more than you'd think.

Because tourists come over on the ferry for day trips and they don't bring a car."

"What does that have to do with me spending the summer at Bainbridge Youth Theater?" I ask.

"What your father's trying to say"—for some reason Mom reaches over and takes the dinner roll from Papa—"is that because money is tight, we can't afford all the activities you usually do in the summer. All your dance classes," she says to Lulu, "and tae kwon do and Science Kidz," she says to me.

Wait, no Science Kidz? But the summer is when we take the ferry from Bainbridge into Seattle and have a sleepover in the Pacific Science Center! And I was about to test for my orange belt in tae kwon do!

"We're really sorry." Papa looks as heartbroken as I feel. "It's not just the activities. It's that I'll always need access to the car, for driving shifts."

"There's just no way we can get you both all over the island and to our jobs," Mom says. "But you can do as many shows and classes at the theater as you want! Always! And because of our current situation, I guarantee you'll be cast!"

Lulu shrugs. "Okay."

Sure, it's okay for her! She only takes dance classes to improve her chances of getting cast in musicals. All she really wants is to perform in a spotlight, just like everyone else in this house.

Except me.

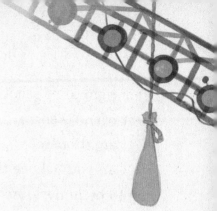

3

No Climbing on the Lighting Grid

I am perched on the catwalks above the stage, and my heart is pounding like Valentina Tereshkova when she realized her spacecraft was programmed to go up but not come back down. My heart's intergalactic drumbeat isn't because I'm hanging out a bunch of feet off the ground, even though if I fell I would splat onto the stage and break probably all of my bones. I've been up here lots of times. It's actually the best place to calm me down after what I just endured.

What I just endured was pretty much the worst thing I have ever done in my entire life. And I've been on the roller coaster at the Washington State

Fair right after a hot dog eating contest with my best friend, Zach.

I auditioned.

Can you believe that? First my mother forces me to be in her dumb show, and then she makes me audition. Even though she guarantees I'll be cast, which I don't want to be anyways! Parents.

"You only have to try, Zadie," Mom said. "Get up there, get through sixteen bars of a song, and you're done."

Like it's that easy?!

I think someone should take a clue from the fact that songs are measured in bars. Like prison bars?

I threatened to sing the song from *Les Misérables* where the prisoners are complaining about how miserable their lives are, but it backfired because Mom said fine, sing that. But I don't know the words, and I definitely wasn't going to learn them.

Lulu said to sing "Happy Birthday," and I hate taking her suggestions, but I couldn't come up with anything else. So Papa played for me while I practiced, and I made everyone else leave the room because it was bad enough with only him right there. It's not that I cared if I was good. But I didn't want to be awful.

Singing "Happy Birthday" should have been easy, right? I've probably sung it at least nine million times. But I got up on that stage when it was my turn and I looked out into the auditorium, and Zach gave me a thumbs-up, and even Lulu gave me a big smile and made a hand motion that could have been a beautiful song coming out of her mouth—or else projectile vomit—and Miss Vanda started playing the piano. A lot faster than Papa when we were practicing, I would like to point out.

And I stood there.

"Zadie, hon?" Mom said from her seat halfway back in the auditorium.

Someone in the audience snickered.

"Let's be respectful," Mom said in her teacher-tone, and can we talk for a minute about how weird it is when it's your mom or dad who's the teacher figure? It's weird.

I guess that's all I have to say about that.

"Let's give it another go," Miss Vanda said. She

played the intro again, a little slower this time at least, and then she softly sang the first few words to help get me going.

But I couldn't make a single note come out. All I could think about was how strange the theater looked from this angle. So boring, to look out and see nothing but rows and rows of seats.

"Zadie?" Mom had come down the aisle and was leaning onto the edge of the stage. "Honey? Are you okay?"

I finally got words out then. Here's what I said: "I can't!"

Then I ran off the stage and climbed up onto the catwalk, and now I can finally breathe. No fear, no limits.

This is the view I like, where I can see everything as part of a bigger whole. Astronauts call it the Overview Effect—seeing Earth as not just that blue-and-green marble you live on, but part of the wider universe.

Theater's not everything, despite what everyone else in my family thinks. It's not that I hate the theater. I like watching it just fine. But it's so much more interesting when I can see what's happening onstage, but also what's happening in the audience, and backstage, and most of all up here, where, if I use that imagination Mom's so fond of, I can pretend I'm not in a theater at all, but I've broken free of Earth's atmosphere and I'm hanging out among the stars.

"Hello," I hear a familiar voice proclaim. "My name is Lourdes Gonzalez"—like absolutely everyone watching doesn't know my sister's name and that her mother is the artistic director, but that's Lulu for you—"and I'm going to be singing 'Sixteen Going on Seventeen.'"

Calmer now, I peer down to see my sister turn to Miss Vanda and nod triumphantly. Normally I'd roll my eyes, but right about now I have more respect for Lulu and her auditioning skills than I ever did before. Still, Lulu is twelve going on seventeen. She wants to play the villain of this show—a fairy-tale mash-up called *Spinderella*—which is an adult character, so she's out to show how mature she is. I don't know why she thinks that's going to happen with a song that includes the words "I need someone older and wiser telling me what to do," but nobody asked me.

Just like nobody asked me if I wanted to spend my entire summer cooped up inside the theater.

She's good, even if the song's totally ridiculous. She's so good that I want to see not only Lulu but also the faces of the people in the audience, so I creep off the catwalk and onto the lighting grid. My mother would freak if she saw me, since the catwalk is a solid three feet wide, but the grid is, well, a grid of metal bars that the lights get fastened onto. It's like a jungle gym, except it's way high off the ground.

But Mom's not going to notice me. All eyes are on Lulu right now. I can see that from the intersection of bars where I've perched. She's really, really good. Even better now that I know how terrifying auditioning is. I need to lean out an inch farther to see my mom's face, and when I do, my hands slip a little on the bar they're gripping.

More than a little. Oh space junk.

As they slip, I realize in slow motion there's a reason Mom would freak if she saw me on the grid: as much as I'd rather be up in zero-G, gravity is very real on this here planet. I could absolutely fall splat to the stage and break all the bones in my body. That might be an effective way to avoid being cast in the show, but there are some obvious downsides.

I lose my grip completely and scramble as I fall, my heart pounding as I try desperately to grab onto something—anything. My body is on a path toward the stage, whether I want to go there or not. (I do not.)

One hand wraps around a nearby metal bar, and then the other hand does too, but in all the flailing, my legs have lost their perch. I madly thrash my legs in an attempt to hoist myself onto the grid, and I've gotten my arms over the bar and one leg hooked over another bar when I realize Lulu is no longer singing. The piano player is no longer playing. There is no sound whatsoever in the whole theater.

Until suddenly there is an explosion of sound.

Lulu is first. "Mom! It's Zadie!"

Miss Vanda leaps up and screams. Then there is the sound of every person in the theater hauling themselves out of their creaky seats and rushing into positions to see me.

This is the next sound I hear: "Zadie Louise Gonzalez, what are you doing?!"

And here's what I say: "Um."

17

Then I hear a bunch of commotion on the ground. I'm not doing a lot of looking down, because (1) while I would fight anyone who said otherwise, it turns out I'm not that strong, and it's taking everything I have to hang on, and (b) while I am not usually afraid of heights, the very real possibility of breaking probably all my bones has me keenly aware of the height at which I dangle.

"Hang on, Zadie," I hear Mr. Cho, the maintenance guy, say.

Hanging on is pretty much my whole life plan right now.

There is a lot of movement down below me, but not enough to drown out Lulu complaining that her audition was interrupted. As though I did this on purpose!

"Okay, Zadie," Mr. Cho says, and his voice is closer now. "I'm right behind you. On a ladder. I could boost you up onto the grid, or steady you down to the ladder. What'll it be?"

"Down! She needs to come down now!" Mom calls. "She shouldn't have been up there in the first place!"

Now does not seem like the time to point out

that I have spent hours on the lighting grid and never fallen through before.

"You heard your mother," Mr. Cho says, and then I feel his hands on my waist. "The top of the ladder is a couple of inches beneath your toes. You're going to have to trust me and let go of the grid."

Do I trust Mr. Cho and the rickety old ladder that's probably been around as long as the theater building, which is an actual Bainbridge Island Historic Site, which means it's a jillion years old? No, I do not.

But this is what I say: "Okay, Mr. Cho." Because sometimes you have to choose your battles.

4
No Quitting an Audition Partway Through

The ride from the theater to our house is less than ten minutes. Eight when Mom is really extra peeved about something, like, say, an actor who still doesn't know their lines at dress rehearsal, or a red crayon that went through the wash cycle with the angel costumes. Or a daughter who crashed through the lighting grid mid-auditions.

Eight minutes doesn't seem like very much time. But you might be surprised how many things my mom can rant about in the time it takes to get from Bainbridge Youth Theater to our street.

To be fair, she saved her ranting for the car.

At the theater, she was all concerned mother and just-glad-I-was-okay and even shared some of the M&M's from the (not) secret stash in her bag's hidden pocket while I sat next to her for the rest of auditions.

She only asked me once why I was up on the grid. I told her it calms me down to be up high, and I was freaking out after my failed audition. She looked like she was about to cry and didn't say anything else.

Little did I know she was saving it all for the car.

I'm going to spare you some of it. You don't need to hear about how dangerous it was and how I'm lucky I didn't break my neck, because you've probably heard that speech before. I'll also skip the part about how, as her daughter, I need to set an example, because none of that makes any logical sense. I'm not even a part of the theater!

"You have put me in an extraordinarily difficult position, Zadie!" She was still going when we passed Frog Rock, and I figured today I probably shouldn't stick my tongue out at the two giant boulders stacked on top of each other and painted like a frog. "You know I need you to be a part of this production. But obviously I'm not going to force you to do something that upsets you so much you go off and put yourself in terrible danger! But where does that leave me? And how was that your solution? The lighting grid? Why not the booth? That's high up!"

I do like the booth. But not as much as the grid. The booth feels like I'm in a rocket ship. The grid feels like I'm on a space walk.

"I mean, Zadie Louise Gonzalez, did you really believe it was all right? Did you really think I would be okay with that? I don't care how upset you were; you understand basic safety and right from wrong!"

Lulu snorts. She's just mad she never got to finish her audition.

I'm the first one through the door when we get home, which means I'm also the first one to be slammed with the smell of Grandma soaking fish in lye—this horrible chemical process to make lutefisk, a Scandinavian delicacy from her youth.

She's dancing around to the rousing sound

of Papa's piano student in the living room, like the smell isn't burning her face off. Grandma's making the best of the racket, probably inventing new moves for her Zumba classes, and she adds an extra shoulder shimmy when we walk in.

"My best girls are home!"

Lulu heads toward Grandma for a hug, but Grandma holds up her chemical-covered gloved hands. "Sorry, sugar," she says. "I probably shouldn't touch you just now."

Mom stalks through the kitchen, muttering, "Of course you're making lutefisk today."

I'm the only one acting halfway normal, and I'm the one who almost died!

By the time Papa's student has left and we sit down to eat (and I've opened all the windows to air out the smell of fish and chemicals), Grandma and Papa have both heard Mom's and Lulu's versions of today. I haven't bothered with my version, because frankly I'm a little annoyed no one seems at all worried about me. I'm pretty sure I'm going to have bruises under my armpits, where I was dangling over the metal bar. And also maybe a traumatic fear of heights (unless that means I can never climb up anything fun again, in which case I'll get over it).

"It sounds like she made a memorable entrance," Grandma says with a twinkle in her eye.

"During my audition! You don't enter during someone else's audition!"

"All right, amor," Papa says, reaching across Mom for the mashed potatoes, instead of asking, which is his first mistake. His second mistake is saying this: "But she got up there on the stage, at least." He turns to me. "You tried something scary, Z. I'm proud of you."

"Scary?" Mom explodes. "Scary was seeing my daughter dangling from the lighting grid! Scary is even now thinking I could get a call from the board tonight, firing me for incompetence! And where would we be then? Without my paycheck? My health insurance?"

I freeze, my spoonful of potatoes stopped halfway to my mouth by a look in my mom's eyes I've never seen before.

"Space explorers aren't the only people who take risks, Zadie Louise. They're not the only ones who make choices and calculations, who are responsible for other people. You're so focused on what else is out there, but do you ever think about the people who are right here with you on this planet?"

5

No Complaining About the Size of Your Role

The next morning, Mom sits me down at the kitchen table, clutching a mug of coffee like it's her last oxygen tank.

"First of all," she says. "I apologize for losing my temper at dinner last night. I wasn't fair to you. I was very, very frightened when you fell yesterday, and I'm heartbroken that the idea of doing theater is so horrifying that you had to flee up there in the first place. I lost control of myself. I'm sorry."

I don't want to meet her eyes, because then I'll have to think about what she said last night.

Could she really have lost her job because of me? I kind of wish I had a mug of coffee to stare into, but coffee is disgusting.

"I'm sorry too." Except the thing is, I'm not sure what I'm sorry for. For making my mom so upset, I guess. Because I'm not sorry I went onto the grid. I've been up there a million times, and this time there was a mishap, but I turned out to be fine. And I can't be sorry I don't want to perform, either. I mean, I wish I did. It would be so much simpler! But it's just not me.

"I'm not going to force you to be in the cast," she says. "And you know how I feel about kids doing tech."

I do. I've heard Mom's diatribe against kids doing tech infinity times. Or maybe more like four, but once was honestly enough.

This is the short version: the technical elements of theater—costumes, sets, lights, sound, and props—are extremely essential parts of the theatrical experience and require very specific training to be done properly and in a way that will not endanger the actors on the stage, and it is far more work and effort to supervise kids doing tech than to hire the few adults who know what they're doing.

That maybe didn't seem like the short version, but trust me, it was.

"But the fact is, you have to spend the summer at the theater. That's just our reality. We don't have any other choices. I'm sorry."

I nod. As much as I hate the idea, it's scary when parents are stressed about money, and I don't want to make it worse than it already is. I'll just bring books and talk to Zach on break and try to stay out of everyone's way, I guess.

"But I can't just leave you unsupervised," she says. "Especially not after the lighting grid."

Or maybe not.

"So you'll be kept busy. Not doing tech, per se. But helping around the theater with whatever needs doing. No lighting grid. No questionable choices. Nothing you haven't been asked directly to do. Got it?"

Because at least I don't have to act, and because I don't want to see Mom's face look like it did last night ever again, I nod. "Got it.

When Mom posts the cast list, she makes Lulu

go online to find out her part like everyone else. No Special Treatment still applies to some parts of this show process, I guess. Lulu screams so loud I know she got the part she'd been practicing forever: Grizelda, Spinderella's evil cousin. It's a bigger, better part than Spinderella, really, considering Spinderella lies there asleep for half the play. And Lulu definitely has the evil cackle down.

Considering the number of times she and Papa have gone through Grizelda's big number in our tiny house, I know this all too well.

When we get to the theater for the first rehearsal, kids are already huddled around the entrance, chattering in excited voices about who got what part. Lulu gets lots of congratulations, and some of them even mean it.

I go to the bathroom because Mom and Lulu rushed me out the door so fast I didn't have time before we left the house. The bathroom backstage is super dinky and kinda cruddy, but the lobby one is usually decent. Which is why I'm surprised to see a cockroach scuttling across the linoleum as I'm sitting there doing my thing.

I don't scream like Lulu would, though. Not because she's some kind of wimp, but because she has a thing about bugs so serious that she refused to even audition when BYT did *James and the Giant Peach*. My mom would probably stomp on it. But I watch him go. Cockroaches are survivors. They can survive, like, outer space. (There actually was a cockroach named Nadezhda who went into outer space in 2007 and laid eggs, which hatched thirty-three baby cockroaches back on Earth. Which must have been a big bummer for them, to start out all weightless and then get born on this planet where gravity holds you down no matter how much you want to float.)

But there's only one cockroach in the bathroom, not thirty-three, and if it can survive where there's no food or sunshine or entertainment, I guess I can survive one summer without my favorite activities. It's not like I have a choice.

When I head back out to the theater, I look for Zach to congratulate him on getting cast as King Horace. But he's always late to everything, and today isn't any different. So I pick a spot in the back of the theater and slump into a seat, looking longingly up at the lighting grid. Even after I almost broke all my bones, I'd rather be up there than down here.

Maddie and Blair are sitting across the aisle from me. They're summer squatters—living in Seattle during the school year but spending the summer on Bainbridge at their island homes.

Blair's sniffling, and Maddie's got an arm around her. "You are so much better than Lulu," Maddie says. "It doesn't make any sense."

"It's not fair!" Blair says, and then shoots daggers at me when she catches me looking, like I had anything to do with anything.

"It's only because her mom's the director," Maddie says, her volume knob swiveling up because she totally knows I can hear her.

I'm not saying anything, because actor drama has nothing to do with me, even if I'm starting to get a prickly feeling in my stomach. But then Lulu walks up to them and says, "Congratulations, you guys! The two queens are really fun parts!"

Blair sneers at her. "Easy for you to say."

Lulu steps back, like Blair's words actually shoved her a little. My sister has spent years

31

getting smaller parts than she deserved, and she's probably trying to be nice because she knows how they feel.

"I'm sorry," Lulu says. "Did I do something to upset you guys?"

Blair starts full-on crying then and runs off toward the bathroom. I hope the cockroach eats her.

"Oh, nothing much." Maddie stands to face Lulu in the aisle. "Only convinced your mom to give you Blair's part."

Maddie turns to go and Lulu's blinking back her own tears and I can't help myself, I really can't.

"She didn't," I call out. "The thing is, our mom likes to give people challenges, and playing an evil witch would come too easily to you two."

I'm not sure who's more shocked—Maddie or Lulu—but right then Mom calls everyone to the stage.

Maddie glares at me. "Talk about not belonging here," she mutters as she stalks away.

Lulu's eyes are still bugged out, looking at me like she's seeing her first extraterrestrial.

"Go on," I say. "Aren't you supposed to go up there?"

It's starting to get weird that Zach's not here by now. I head down the aisle to grab Mom's phone and text him. Which was a mistake, because Mom notices me and beckons me onto the stage.

"You too, Zadie," she says. "All-company meeting!"

Oh space junk.

But it's not really. If it were an all-company meeting, Mrs. Freymiller, the costume designer, would be here. And Fiona, who does sets and props. But not our long-time lighting designer, Grandpa Bob, who's not my grandpa, or anyone else's that I know of, but who everyone's called Grandpa Bob forever. He retired to Arizona after the last show, and I don't know who's designing lights this time.

I trudge up the stairs on the side of the stage. I've been to lots of first rehearsals, but I've always been looking down from the grid, or listening from underneath the trapdoor, or watching from behind the dark glass of the booth. I've never been on the stage with all these kids who actually want to be up here, and who look at my mom like she's some kind of superhero.

(She is not.)

Since Zach isn't here, I sit in between a new boy with spiky green hair and Olivia, an islander who always plays small parts but is never rude about it.

"Marinee, Blair's in the bathroom," Maddie calls out as Mom motions for everyone to sit down.

"That's all right. Blair's heard this opening speech a few times," Mom says. "For those of you who are new, though, always let me or the stage manager know if you're running to the bathroom during rehearsal. There's one in the lobby, and one backstage.

"Speaking of the stage manager, we've got someone new who I'm very excited about. I think you're all going to really like her. She missed her ferry, but she'll be here soon, and I know you'll give her the same respect you give me."

Maddie raises her hand but calls out again without waiting to be recognized. "What's Zadie doing here? She wasn't on the cast list."

Mom takes a breath. "Zadie is . . . helping out."

"Doing tech? I thought kids didn't do tech at BYT."

"Thank you, Maddie. She's not doing tech. Let's call her . . . an assistant producer."

Assistant producer? I actually kind of like the sound of that.

Mom gets back to her opening speech—all the boring rule stuff. For something supposedly so fun, there are an awful lot of rules. Don't be late. Don't tell other actors what to do. Don't move someone else's prop. No electronics in the theater. No jumping off the apron.

"What's the apron?" asks a tiny kid with a shocking amount of freckles.

"Good question," Mom says. "The apron is this front part of the stage. It's close enough to the ground to be tempting, but it's far enough for twisted ankles, or worse. The stairs on either side of the stage are there for a reason."

"Can we jump off the apron in an emergency? Like if there's a fire or an earthquake or a tsunami?"

Mom blinks at this kid for a second. Then she

says, "An emergency is all the more reason to follow rules. Mostly, I want you to use good judgment. Sometimes things go wrong or mistakes get made. We can talk about those! But there's no wiggle room on the safety issues. Absolutely no jumping off the apron."

She starts to talk about how there are no small parts, only small actors, and I know that small actor with the freckles really wants to ask a question about that, too. I don't blame him. I've heard her say it infinity times, but I still think it's totally dumb. There are absolutely, no-doubt-about-it small parts.

There's a reason Blair and Maddie are so prickly.

My mind is kind of wandering, and also my eyes, which is why I notice Blair coming back from the bathroom, slipping into the auditorium from the lobby. She's carrying a clear water bottle out in front of her like it contains toxic gases. I focus my laser eyes on the bottle.

Oh my shooting stars, it *does* have something toxic inside.

Not toxic, I guess, but terrifying to a lot of

people. There's no mistaking the black thing scuttling around inside the bottle. Instead of heading straight down the aisle toward the stage, Blair darts over to a seat with a purple magic sequin backpack on it. Lulu's backpack. Blair unscrews the lid from the bottle.

I see it happening in slow motion, but what my mom sees is me shouting, "Oh no you don't!" while I leap off the edge of the apron.

6

No Kids Allowed in the Booth

Nobody believes me, but Blair was about to drop a cockroach in Lulu's backpack. Blair, who knows exactly how my sister feels about bugs because she got mad when Lulu wouldn't go see her play the Centipede in *James and the Giant Peach*. But then in all the commotion of me jumping off the apron, and Mom yelling, and everyone yelling, Blair dumped the poor cockroach out and held up an empty bottle and swore I was making it all up.

But I'm a terrible actor! And she's supposedly such a good one. Doesn't logic say she's the one lying?

I think Lulu might have believed me. But that

didn't mean she stood up for me when Mom said, in front of everyone, that it was inexcusable to jump off the apron immediately after her safety lecture, and there would be serious consequences.

Like what? Banning me from the theater? I wish!

So now I'm waiting out rehearsal in the booth, where the stage manager sits during shows and controls all the tech. It's dark and cozy and no one comes up here until the week before a show opens, so it's perfect for hiding out and awaiting my doom. There is one corner where the roof leaks when it rains, which is a lot around here, but not so much in summer. And anyway, astronauts have to put up with much more challenging environmental considerations when they're rocketing through space.

I run my hands over the levers that control the lights. It's not as life-and-death as flying a spacecraft, but it might be as intricate. I've sat here, watching stage managers run shows. They have everything at their fingertips, and it's all so logical. You push a lever up, and the lights go on. Press a key on the computer, and the sound goes off. It makes so much more sense than everyone down there, all pretending to be someone they're not.

It makes so much more sense than every member of my family who'd rather be down there on the stage.

"Um, no kids allowed in the booth."

I tell you what: I am not in the mood for someone I've never even seen before telling me I'm not allowed in the booth where I took my first steps. (That might be what my parents call a fabrication, but if I didn't take my first steps in here, I at least had my diaper changed in here.) But one glance at her all-black clothes, no-nonsense ponytail stuck through with pencils, and incredible utility belt, and I know she's the new stage manager.

And she's awesome.

"It's okay," I say. "I'm Marinee's kid."

"I'm Ana María. And there are no kids in my booth."

I get up, and she immediately sets down her Oregon Shakespeare Festival tote on the chair.

"You've been to Ashland?"

Lulu's been begging Mom to take her to the

Oregon Shakespeare Festival since she could recite her first lines from the Bard. (You'd think they might have been something easy, like "To be or not to be." But because Lulu is Lulu, she memorized some complicated thing with a bunch of rhyming.)

I have no interest in the Shakespeare Festival, but Oregon is one of the top states in the country for UFO sightings—crop circles, flying saucers, you name it. If we ever go to Ashland, I'm hoping for mid-May, and then I'll sneak out and hitch a ride to McMinnville, Oregon, which hosts an annual UFO Fest. Three whole days of parades, guest speakers, and other people who believe there has to be more out there than earthly humanity.

Ana María considers me for a second, and a seed of hope sprouts inside. "I worked there for the last two years," she says.

"As stage manager?"

"ASM and master electrician."

Master electrician at a massive theater festival like OSF! Finally, someone who must get my love for the grid. A master electrician practically lives up there. Maybe Ana María is the solution to this whole messed-up summer. If I had to do tech, it'd be lights, and here she is: an expert with wisdom to share. Next stop: the universe!

I sink onto the stool in the far corner. "I'll be so quiet you won't know I'm here."

"Nope," she says, pulling her laptop from her bag. It's covered in stickers. Rainbows and roller skates and NO HUMAN IS ILLEGAL. And . . . is that a NASA logo?! But before I can ask, she insists, "No kids in my booth."

"I believe Zadie," Lulu says that night when I'm supposed to be taking a bath, but instead I am crouching out of sight in the hallway and listening to Mom and Papa discuss My Behavior. "Blair is awful, and she's had it out for me forever. Plus she really wanted to be cast as Grizelda."

"Blair has been a part of Bainbridge Youth Theater since you were both literal Munchkins! She has never been in trouble, not once. Your sister, on the other hand . . ."

Sir Andrew Lloyd Webber finds me in the hallway and plops down in front of me, expecting pets.

"Okay, but there's such a thing as kids who do stuff they should get in trouble for, but don't."

My heart swells with love for Lulu. It's weird.

"I am aware of that, Lourdes, but I also think I'm fairly aware of what's going on at the theater."

It takes everything I have not to snort. Mom does her best, but even she gets suckered by the kiss-ups. Sir Andrew Lloyd Webber bats at the hand that stopped petting him.

"I'm just saying," Lulu says. "But now I'm going to work on my lines, if that's okay."

"Of course, honey."

I should probably get back to the bathroom, but it seems like Lulu's on my side, so I stay put. Chances are good she won't rat me out this time. She rolls her eyes when she sees me in the hallway but says nothing. The cat follows her into our room.

"I'm at a loss," Mom says to Papa. "Anyone else blatantly doing something immediately after I've strictly forbidden it? They'd be removed from the program. If the island council heard . . . I can't risk them thinking that the theater could be liable when kids—"

"Okay, take a breath," Papa says. "Bainbridge is small, but not so small the council will hear every time a kid takes a tumble at the youth theater."

"But it wasn't even an accident. She dove! And now I have the bigger question of what to do with her. I thought she could help out, but the new stage manager doesn't want her skulking around and I am not risking losing Ana María. She's way overqualified as it is. Did I tell you she's a master electrician?"

"Cielo," Papa says. "Sit down. Zadie is a good kid. Surely this isn't as big a disaster as it feels like right now."

"It is!" she wails. "It's a massive disaster!"

She thinks I'm a disaster? Even with all the yelling and lectures, this is a death ray to the gut. She doesn't only think I'm the weirdo daughter who doesn't share her love of performance and will never be able to relate to her. She thinks I'm out to ruin everything.

I have to prove her wrong.

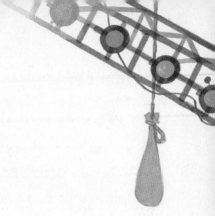

7
Stay Hydrated

I'm going to spend the whole summer at the theater. That's just a fact, like the speed of light (299,792,458 miles per second). If I'm going to survive, I have to accomplish a couple of things. First, I have to be helpful in ways that don't make Mom think I'm out to sabotage the whole production. If I can do the first one, maybe I can win over Ana María and convince her to actually teach me something about lights. Which would get me back up on the grid.

I brainstormed ways to accomplish these goals for hours last night, and this is all I came up with:

- Get rid of the roaches in the bathroom. (Ew.)
- Fold the mailers in the lobby. (Boring.)
- Spy on Blair and Maddie to make sure they don't *actually* sabotage the production. (Perfect.)

The next morning, I do not get to eavesdrop on Blair and Maddie from underneath the trapdoor like I envisioned while lying awake. Instead, I'm sitting in the lobby, folding flyers and stuffing them into envelopes. (It turns out they don't fit in the envelopes after you've made them into a paper airplane.)

This is about as close to teching lights as selling popcorn at the planetarium is close to being an astronaut. But at least I don't have to make an effort to hear what Blair and Maddie are talking about—they make sure I hear.

"Look at poor Zadie," Blair says. "I almost feel bad for her."

"Yeah, but remember," Maddie says. "There are no small parts, only small actors. Except . . . wait! She's not even an actor, is she?"

They cackle together as they head into the auditorium, and for a second I realize they both could play Grizelda no problem.

"What's with your face?"

My face changes then from whatever scowly thing it was doing into a huge grin. "Zach! Where were you yesterday?"

If Zach had been there for cockroach-palooza, things would have gone down differently. He would have backed me up (whether he saw Blair or not), and Mom would have listened to him, because everyone listens to Zach, even adults. Or maybe he would have told Blair and Maddie to chill out before the cockroach thing even happened.

He sighs. "My dads got confused about the schedule. They're so busy with the twins that they couldn't keep track of when rehearsals started."

"That's weird." Zach's been doing shows at BYT forever, and his dads know the drill. But they do have a lot going on, what with their four—now six—kids.

"Yeah, who knew building an addition to the house while also fostering new toddler twins would be hectic?"

"You're still getting your own room, right?"

"The attic! I told Pop your idea about a sky-light so we can watch the stars during sleepovers, and he said it'll have to wait until the addition is finished."

"Bummer."

"Yeah. I heard things got pretty crazy here yesterday. You jumped off the apron?"

"I had my reasons."

"I know. The roach thing. Talk about sore losers."

"They're not even losers. They got really good parts. You're happy as the king, right? They're the queens!"

"I know, it's dumb. I get feeling jealous, but they're taking it too far." He narrows his eyes. "What I don't get is why you care. I'd think you'd be joining forces with them."

Lulu is the only sensitive spot between Zach and me. He's my best friend, but he's got the stupidest crush on my perfect sister, and he gets all bent out of shape when he thinks I'm not worshipping Her Highness enough.

For a second, though, I consider the question. Why *do* I care? Lulu annoys me more than anyone. She thinks the world revolves around her and her theatrical aspirations. She's always locking me out of our room so she can practice lines or dance routines or who knows what else. I should be collecting cockroaches for Blair to dump in her backpack.

But Lulu's spent years in small roles, mostly so Mom doesn't look like she's giving her daughter the best parts, and she worked really hard for the part of Grizelda. I respect that. Plus she stuck up for me last night.

"I just do, okay? Look, I need you to keep an eye on Blair and Maddie during rehearsals. I can't spy from the grid anymore."

"It'll cost you."

I roll my eyes. Zach would pay *me* for an excuse to watch out for Lulu. "What do you want?"

"Gummies. Gummy bears. Gummy snakes. Gummy toilets. I don't care. Gimme the gummies."

"What do you need me for? You're the candy king!"

I'm not ashamed to admit that I became

friends with Zach for his candy collection. I mean, it turned out he was fun to hang out with too. But mostly, I knew the candy stashes in his closet could supply the International Space Station for decades.

Zach flashes a kind of crazed grimace at me and points at his braces. "They've taken my gummies! Also my gum and toffees and caramels. Jelly beans, jawbreakers, you name it!"

"What about your hiding spots?"

"Dad found them when we were moving my stuff up to the attic. Most of them, anyway. The chocolate selection is secure. But I would punch a baby for anything gummy right now."

At my look of alarm Zach grins, genuine this time. "Not really. Arlo and Penny are safe from me. They might be screwing up the household schedule, but it's not their fault."

I know Zach would help me look out for Lulu whether I fulfilled his demands or not. But fair's fair. "Deal," I say. "I'll be your gummy source, and you'll keep an eye on the evil not-sisters."

"Deal."

••●••

By the time the flyers are all folded and stuffed, I have more paper cuts than fingers. But I've definitely been helpful, and I'm looking forward to an afternoon spent curled up under the stage, very carefully turning the pages of my *Women in Aerospace* book.

Instead, Ana María appears in the lobby, hauling a plastic storage tub.

"Zadie, right?"

I jump up. "That's me! Did you change your mind? I can help with whatever you want!"

"Great." She hoists the tub onto the table I just cleared of flyers and envelopes. "You can set up the snack. They'll be out in twenty minutes."

Snack duty?! I tell you what: that is not a step up from flyers. But maybe I can show Ana María I'm a team player, here to support the production. I not-so-casually rotate my *Women in Aerospace* book on the table so she can see it clearly. She has a NASA sticker, after all. Surely if she understood we're kindred spirits—

"Don't spill anything," she snaps as she strides away. "We've already got roaches."

So much for kindred spirits.

I open the bin, crossing my fingers for fruit snacks. I'm planning to snag extras for Zach, but my heart sinks. Raisins and graham crackers? There isn't even juice! Only those really squatty bottles of water. Which are terrible for the planet, by the way.

Grumbling to no one except maybe the cockroaches, I start arranging things on the table. Two crackers and a box of raisins on each napkin. I'm laying out the last one when the doors from the theater burst open and the cast of *Spinderella* descends.

"Water's in the bin!" I shout over the hordes of kids grabbing their snacks.

Blair pulls out a water bottle in distaste. "These are so bad for the environment," she says.

I scowl at her, even though I had the exact same thought. "Then bring your own."

"Graham crackers and raisins?" Aidan wrinkles his nose. "What, are we in kindergarten?"

"I, for one, enjoy a good graham cracker and raisin pairing," Zach booms. "I like to think of them as ants on a field of dirt."

Blair rolls her eyes and drags Maddie and

Aidan off to their own corner. But a bunch of kids crowd around Zach as he dumps his raisins out on top of his graham cracker and starts eating them with gusto.

Thank goodness for Zach. He's going to earn every gummy I can get for him.

8

Assume the Director Is Always Watching

The week does not improve.

Whenever I offer to do something actually tech-related, like help Ana María pull down the lights that need new bulbs, or even costume stuff, like helping to spray-paint the cardboard crowns, I get shut down like a rocket out of fuel.

"I work alone," Ana María says.

"Go set up snack," Mom says.

Whenever I find somewhere to curl up and read, or draw, or use old backdrops to build a Soyuz capsule, someone yells that I'm in the way.

Zach has nothing interesting to report about

Blair and Maddie, either. Not that I want them to be up to something. It's better for Lulu if they've chilled out. But still, I wouldn't object to an eensy bit of sabotage.

When we get home on Friday, Papa's sitting with his head in his hands at the kitchen table, surrounded by papers. A pot of beans simmers on the stove, but even the familiar smell doesn't look like it's comforting him.

"What are you doing?" I plop down across from him while Mom and Lulu beeline to their rooms, tired of interacting with people all day.

"Filling out all the paperwork to drive for Ryde."

"Don't you just have to . . . drive?" I pull some of the papers toward me—car registration, insurance, background checks.

"They have to make sure I'm a safe driver. Which I understand! I'd just rather be making music, you know?"

I definitely know about doing boring busy-work instead of what you want to be doing.

"How about we make the tortillas?" he says,

gathering the papers into a pile and standing up. "Wash your hands."

"Won't the germs get cooked out anyway?" I ask.

Papa shoots me a grin that means, "Do it anyway because your mom will ask if you did." "Just wash 'em quick.

"So how's it going for you, mija?" he asks as he pulls the bowl of masa from the fridge and starts to roll it into balls.

I ponder how honest to be as I pull the tortilla press from the cupboard. I'm terrible at making tortillas, but I love doing it. First, you make a ball of the squishy dough, like you're playing with clay. Then, if you're super talented like the ladies who sell tortillas in Guatemala, where Papa's from, you slap the ball between your hands a few times, and cosmic awesomeness! The ball transforms into a flat sort of pancake, which you toss down onto the hot pan.

My tía Elsa tried to teach me once, and it did not go well. But if you are not super talented with the tortilla dough, that's okay too. Then you get to use the tortilla press, which is honestly so satisfying that I don't mind not being able to do it authentically. You set the ball of dough on the center of the press, and then you use this lever thing to squash a heavy metal plate down on top of it. When you lift it up again, a perfect tortilla is ready for the pan!

"Are you keeping busy at the theater?" Papa asks, handing me a ball of dough.

I almost groan but then quickly sneak a peek at the doorway to make sure Mom isn't listening. If she hears me complain at all, I'll get the most annoying lecture about how at least she's not making me perform. Which: okay. But boring busywork is not the same thing as doing real tech like hanging lights, and it's definitely not spending the summer at the planetarium. But I know from experience that the lecture will only get longer if I point that out.

"I'm pretty bored." I push the lever down so hard that the dough squishes out the sides of the tortilla press. I knew that would happen, and it would make the tortilla unusable, but sometimes you've got to do something whether it's a good idea or not.

Papa doesn't even scold me, like Mom would.

He opens the press and scrapes the dough back together into a fresh ball.

"What sort of things are you doing?"

"Sweeping the lobby and folding programs."

Papa takes the new tortilla I pressed and flips it onto the pan. "I'm really sorry you're missing Science Kidz. And everything you like to do, Z."

He looks so sad I immediately feel like a giant slug. It isn't his fault he's such a good teacher that his music students are moving on to actual music careers!

"It's okay, Papa." I make another ball of dough. I always make them too big, but he doesn't care. "I'm okay. I'm having fun."

But the thing is, we all know I'm an absolute-no-doubt-about-it terrible actor. There's no way he believes me.

After dinner I offer to help with the dishes, because I still feel bad about before. But Grandma Sooz shoos me out of the kitchen, saying she needs to talk to my parents about boring adult stuff.

Normally, that'd be enough to send me outside with the telescope I found at a garage sale that's

not the best but it's better than nothing. Grandma Sooz never makes up excuses to get rid of me. When she says she needs to talk about boring stuff, it usually has to do with her Zumba studio—taxes or advertising or whatever. Definitely boring.

But something makes me hang back. Not all the way—I don't stay in the kitchen. I stop in the hall and wait. Just to see. Lately, the boring adult stuff has had big kid consequences, like me getting stuck at the theater all day, every day.

"All right, kids," Grandma says to Mom and Papa. "We have to have this conversation."

"Mom, no," my own mom says. "I've already told you—"

"Well, I want to hear from Felipe, too. We're all family in this house."

Mom lets out the exasperated huff she usually only uses on me.

That's when our bedroom door cracks open, and Lulu peeks out. I glare at her, warning her not to give me up or I will spit in her rehearsal raisins. But she tiptoes out and slides down the wall next to me.

"What's on your mind, Sooz?" Papa sounds

like he just returned to Earth from orbit and the gravity is dragging him down.

"Let's cut to the chase. We all know you kids could bring in a really decent rent on the basement apartment," Grandma starts.

"We are not taking rent from you!"

"I'm not offering!" Grandma retorts, and I stifle a giggle. "I can't afford what you could charge on that place—"

"Well, there's not room for you to move into the house. The piano takes up half the living room, the girls already share a room, and—"

"Would you zip it up and let me tell you what I'm thinking?"

This time Papa's the one who chuckles, but I guarantee you steam is coming out of Mom's ears.

"Fine, Mother," she says.

"My friend Arlene," Grandma goes on, "is the activities director at a retirement home. She has offered me a position there, running the fitness program. In exchange, I'd get a lovely studio apartment, rent-free."

I gasp, and Lulu reaches out to grab my hand. She isn't telling me to be quiet. She's upset too. Sure, we're all a little crowded in this house. Our

kitchen is barely big enough for one person to make a meal; with three adults and two kids bustling about, it's basically impossible. Sir Andrew Lloyd Webber doesn't help matters, always weaving around underfoot.

With Grandma living in the basement, there's no storage space for other stuff, so we can't even keep the cars in the garage, since that's where we keep the lawn mower and suitcases and stuff like that.

And we all share one bathroom, which, if I'm being honest, is the worst part of a small house.

But I wouldn't change any of that if it means Grandma would live somewhere else. Grandma Sooz—the only person in this family who gets me at all!

The tortillas and beans in my stomach are a giant hunk of space rock. I have to do something—race into the kitchen and convince Grandma she can't ever live anywhere but right here on Bainbridge Island, in our house, her home—but I'm frozen. Then Lulu gasps again.

"What?" Did I miss something?

"Did you hear that?" she whispers. "Her friend Arlene lives in *Florida*."

9
Don't Touch Someone Else's Prop

"So, Zadie," Mom says on the way to the theater on Monday morning. I narrow my eyes at the back of the driver's seat. I've been waiting all weekend for someone to say something about Grandma's proposal on Friday night.

But no, they carry on as though our entire family isn't about to implode like a space shuttle passing through Earth's atmosphere without a heat shield. Papa makes goofy jokes while preparing his morning smoothie. Grandma tries to get me to salsa with her on her way out the door. And now Mom's using a super-weird, chipper voice.

"Papa and I were talking last night."

Finally. I straighten up. But why is she only addressing me? Lulu is sitting right next to her.

"He has convinced me that I may be wasting your talents at the theater." Lulu snorts. "You've been very helpful, doing the things we've asked you to do. I am willing to give you some more tech-related responsibility if, and only if, there are absolutely no shenanigans. And you stay out of Ana María's way."

She goes on for the rest of the ride, lecturing about Responsibility and Setting a Good Example, but I'm barely listening. She's not letting me up on the grid, and that's the only tech that would interest me. Anyway my mind is too busy orbiting the possibility of Grandma Sooz moving all the way across the country. As if that isn't bad enough (it is), some stranger would rent out the basement!

Anybody could move in! A murderer! A scorpion breeder! A tuba player!

"So do we have a deal?" Mom says as she pulls into the BYT parking lot.

"Yeah, sure," I say. She twists around in her seat after parking and gives me a funny look.

Then she sighs and gets out of the car.

"Why aren't you more excited?" Lulu says. "Costumes are the best tech discipline."

I scramble out of the car to follow after Lulu. Maybe I should have been listening. "What about costumes?"

"Didn't you hear Mom? She said Mrs. Freymiller was supposed to take costume measurements today, but her daughter's baby came early and she can't make it in all week. She asked if you could do it."

Oh my shooting stars! "Take the measurements? Me?!"

Costumes aren't in the same galaxy as lighting, but they're light-years better than folding programs. I can pretend I'm designing space suits to fit female astronauts so they're not kept from space walks because there aren't enough suits to fit them. (This is a real thing that happened.)

"Yeah, and you better not screw it up, because I've seen her sketches, and my costume is going to be amazing."

Lulu ignores Blair and Maddie huddled together by the door and sweeps inside with the flair of Mrs. Freymiller herself, who wears rhinestone-covered glasses and giant, swoopy hats, and long, flowy cardigans in jewel-bright colors. Mrs. F always smells like incense and jam, and she has an intriguing accent I can never quite place.

"Okay." Ana María is totally skeptical as she hands me the clipboard in the overstuffed costume closet. "Have each kid tell you their sizes for the items listed here: shoes, shirts, pants. If they don't know, mark that so we can email their parent to ask. Some need special measurements taken, like waist or arm length, or head circumference if their character wears a crown. Mrs. Freymiller wrote down whatever she needs for each character."

Ana María reaches into her totally awesome tool belt and hands me a measuring tape and a pen. "Don't mess this up," she says.

I will not mess this up. I am Valentina Tereshkova preparing to orbit the earth solo for seventy-one hours. One wrong measurement and I'll spin out into the vastness of space, never to return.

To make things even better, Zach is the first actor Mom sends down.

"What up, Mrs. Frey-zadie?" He looks around the costume closet. "Nice office. This is a way better gig than snack duty."

"I know, right? I mean, it's just costumes, but still." I consult the clipboard. Zach plays King Horace, so I need to get his head circumference for a crown. "Sit down on the stool."

He sits. I pick up the measuring tape, which is like a floppy ruler but way longer, and consider his head.

"Do you know what a circumference is?"

"Bless you," he says.

It's a crown, so even if I'm not sure about circumference, I figure it's a solid guess that they need to know how big his noggin is. I wrap the measuring tape around, trying to decide how to handle Zach's . . . generous ears and finally decide the crown would sit right above them

"Any news from the evil queens?" I ask as I write down the measurement.

"Oh yeah!" Zach twirls on the stool. "I can't believe I forgot! This morning I caught Blair switching out the water in the goblet Lulu drinks from during the feast. Guess what she put in instead?"

My mind explodes with possibilities.

But before I can decide on one, Zach says, "Vinegar!"

"No. Way."

"Way."

"Did you tell my mom?"

"Ana María was right there, so I told her. Blair swore up and down that she was using the vinegar to polish the goblet and was going to refill it with water when she was done. Ana María lectured her about touching other people's props. But still—I stopped her."

That's something, at least. I grab my backpack, stashed under a pile of ball gowns, and dig out a pack of gummy bears for Zach. "Good job. Keep it up."

"Thanks." He rips the bag open right there. "I need the sugar boost. The twins were crying all night."

Several townspeople are next, and they don't need any special measurements since their costumes will just be pulled from stock—the endless jumble of costumes on hand from past shows—so I have them fill out their forms and help them if they don't know their sizes. An eight-year-old should wear a size eight; a ten-year-old should wear a size ten. It's just logic.

When Lulu comes in, she says she'll take her own measurements. She absolutely does not want me to touch her with the measuring tape.

"You'll mess it up," she says. Rude.

I hold up the tape. "I'm not calculating launch trajectory. We learned to measure stuff in kindergarten." She is not convinced. "Look, watch me measure the length of your arm."

She's stiffer than the mannequin staring at us from the corner, but she watches me place one end of the flimsy tape at her shoulder, then smooth it out along the length of her arm and stop at her wrist.

"Sixteen inches," I pronounce triumphantly.

She double checks I'm right and finally relents to let me do the rest of the measurements: hips, waist, bust (this one takes more convincing), and something called armscye, which she insists on googling with the phone she's not even supposed to have. (But it's a good thing she did, because I had no idea there was even a word for the measurement of your armhole!)

The weirdest thing is, when I tell Lulu about Blair and the goblet, she doesn't seem surprised. Mostly she seems sad.

"I don't get it," she says. "I've been disappointed with my role lots of times. It's part of doing theater. That doesn't mean I'd sabotage another actor. Especially someone I considered my friend."

"When Mom hears, she'll definitely kick Blair out, at least."

Lulu freezes. "Mom can't find out. Promise me you won't tell her."

"Why not?"

"Because it'll make everything worse! Maddie would be even more determined to make my life miserable. The next show, Blair would be out for blood. I don't need the stress! I have enough to worry about right now."

Oh space junk. Lulu's eyes are filling up with tears.

If I were her, I'd want revenge. But I can see what she means. If I can't help with the mean-girls issue, I have to help with something. So I say the only other thing that comes to mind, even if I'm not totally confident about it myself. "We're going to find a way to keep Grandma from moving out." I hand her a tissue.

She looks skeptical. "Maybe. That's the worst thing. But also, playing Grizelda is a lot of work." She sinks down onto the stool, even though she's done with her measurements. "I wouldn't give it up, but I didn't realize how much pressure it would be, you know?"

It's weird, but I do know. I felt a lot of pressure when I thought I'd have to be some random background servant. It isn't fair that Lulu has the responsibilities of her part, plus jealous castmates like Blair and Maddie, plus everything happening at home. I thought perfect Lulu was doing perfectly fine, but I can admit when I've miscalculated.

"You earned the part, and you're doing great," I finally say. "I won't tell Mom about Blair and Maddie."

That doesn't mean I won't have Zach on the case, but I keep that to myself.

"Thank you, Z," Lulu says, wiping her eyes and composing herself. "I'm glad Mom trusted you with this job. You're doing great too."

As the other kids come and go from the costume closet, I can't stop thinking about everything that's changed in the last few weeks. None of it is fair, and the worst part is, there's no one to blame. Not really. Mom and Papa are doing the best they can. Grandma Sooz is trying to help by offering to move out. Even Ana María thinks she's doing the best thing for the show by keeping me from helping with tech.

But maybe I'm thinking about it wrong. Maybe I shouldn't be blaming anyone. Grandma Sooz always says, "If you're not part of the solution, you're part of the problem."

So what's the solution? This brainstorming session requires some fuel, so between measurements, I dig out the gummy bears I brought for myself. They're from last Halloween, so they're kind of hard, but I like them better that way. It's like the little bears are putting up more of a fight before letting you gobble them down.

If Mom and Papa had more money, I could do the activities I actually want to do. Lulu would still have the pressure of her role, but it wouldn't be complicated by other worries. And most important, Grandma Sooz wouldn't need to move out.

I stick a finger into my mouth to dislodge a bear that's gotten stuck on a back molar. And that's when it hits me.

Zach's probably not the only kid who needs a sugar boost to get through these days of crackers and raisins. And for the next month, I have access to a whole bunch of kids, lots of whom are island summer squatters, which means their families can afford two houses. If I provide the candy, I bet they'll pay up.

10
Don't Eat in Costume

"Now, what on earth are you going to do with all this candy?" Grandma Sooz asks as Zach helps me haul the last giant tub onto the flat wheely cart and we climb on. Mom always says I'm too big to ride the carts at SaveCo, but Grandma says having my weight on there is good for her muscles. I'm just here to help.

Zach's here because the renovations at his house—not to mention the horde of little kids—are driving him bonkers, and he jumped at the chance to take the ferry with me and Grandma Sooz into Seattle for a SaveCo run.

"I'm going to be entrepreneurial." She'll like that, because I've sat in on her Entrepreneurship for Seniors workshop more than once. (She always has good snacks.) Grandma is a firm believer in spotting business opportunities and making the most of them. That's how she took a Zumba class at the senior center and grew it into her own very successful Zumba studio.

I don't understand how she can even consider giving up everything she's worked so hard for. But nobody asked me.

"Like a lemonade stand, but with candy?"

"Sort of."

Grandma nods. "I can see that. You pay ten dollars for six pounds of licorice in that tub. But there's got to be . . . what? A hundred and fifty pieces? Say you sell them for a quarter a piece, why that's . . ."

While she does the math in her head, I assess what I've found—a tub of licorice, a huge jar of jelly beans, a giant box of gummy snakes, and a massive bag of mini chocolate bars. I'm pretty sure that will last through rehearsals.

"That's thirty-seven dollars and fifty cents!" she exclaims. "That's a profit margin of seventy-three percent!"

I don't know why I didn't think of this sooner. Maybe I can not only keep Grandma Sooz living with us but also earn enough money to get myself back in Science Kidz. I'm investing everything I've saved in my spaceship bank from birthday and Christmas money, and it'll be worth every penny if my mission is successful.

Other grandmas might ask more questions, but Grandma Sooz believes in giving kids the freedom to try and fail (not that I'm going to!), and also to spend their money however they want. Plus I'm counting on the fact that she and Mom are both way too busy to talk to each other anymore.

"That's everything on my list," Grandma says, consulting an actual list on paper instead of a notes app, like a regular grown-up. The cart is piled high with bottles of water and energy bars, which she provides at Zoom Zoom Zumba. It also has a few things Mom and Papa requested for our household, but not much because we don't have the storage for SaveCo quantities. "How about you, Zach?"

He doesn't even have to look at the list to know what his dads asked for. "Diapers."

He hops off and motions for Grandma to take a turn riding. She climbs on with me, ignoring the strange look from a man in a suit who stalks past at that moment, and Zach pushes us over to the aisle filled with baby stuff.

"How are the twins doing?" Grandma asks him.

Zach shrugs. "They scream a lot. But they'll adjust. New kids always do."

Zach's dads have fostered and adopted six kids total now, and Zach's been with them the longest, so he's been there for a lot of household upheaval—Micah's night terrors, Jasmine's seizures, Namina's anger management issues, which resulted in every single one of Zach's Lego creations getting smashed in one horrible night a couple of years ago. He was obviously upset, but even then Zach got that his siblings were going to have some troubles adjusting, considering how hard their lives had been.

(Namina's doing a lot better now. Last time I was at their house, I beat her at Candy Land, and she was as cool as her oldest brother.)

"Your dads are very special people."

Zach stops the cart in front of the diapers and searches for the ones his dads asked for. He doesn't say anything, because he's polite and knows Grandma means well, but I know that annoys him. People say it all the time, but I don't think they realize it makes it sound like Jacob and Jim are these saints who've bestowed this blessing on these poor downtrodden kids, instead of the kids being the blessing and Jacob and Jim being lucky to have them as their family.

I'll tell Grandma later, because she always wants to know when she can do better. But I think it would embarrass Zach if I said anything now. So instead I start loudly counting out my money on top of the giant diaper box as we head to stand in the long lines for checkout.

"I'm really proud of you, Zig-Zag," Grandma says as Zach returns the cart through the misty lot to the store and we arrange the groceries in the trunk of Grandma's car. Some people call this perpetually gray summer weather "June gloom," but I like to think of it as Jupiter's atmosphere with three different layers of clouds.

Grandma hasn't called me Zig-Zag in forever.

It started when I came home from kindergarten crying because three of the girls in my class all had the same initials—Emma Anderson, Emma Arnold, and Esther Atchison—and they had made this huge deal about it and formed the EA club and no one was ever going to have my initials and I'd never be in a club or have any friends ever.

Maybe that's why I liked Zach the minute I met him—another Z-name!

But Grandma Sooz made up a silly song about a zealous, zany zig-zag zebra named Zadie. . . . I don't remember all the words now, but the point was how fun and cool it was to have a name that began with Z. She called me Zig-Zag for that whole year, at least.

There has to be a good reason she's pulling out Zig-Zag now. "Why?"

"The way you've been handling everything lately. Not getting to go to your activities. I know how hard that is for you."

"Oh. Yeah, thanks." Now that I'm worried about her moving across the country, I've barely even been thinking about tae kwon do or Science Kidz. Part of me wants her to bring up the move to Florida. I've always been able to count on Grandma Sooz to be honest with me. But another part of me—a bigger part, if I'm honest with myself—hopes she won't. Because until she does, it won't be real.

And maybe it isn't! When Grandma told Mom and Papa about Florida, it didn't sound like anything had been decided. It was only a possibility. Even if it is decided, it'll probably take a while for her to close down the studio and plan a cross-country move. So if I can get moving on Operation Candy Empire, maybe it will never happen.

Grandma stays in the car on the ferry ride back to the island, but Zach and I climb the stairs from the dark, cramped car deck up to the bright, spacious decks above, where families sit by big windows playing card games, and commuters hunch over laptops, and tourists point out the windows at I don't even know what. Water, I guess.

Zach and I head straight for the outer deck. It's always chilly on the ferry, even in the summer, as the wind whips our hair around our faces. But we lean into it, our arms propped on the rails.

"Sorry about my grandma."

Zach shakes me off. "Your grandma is great."

She really is. "She might be moving," I say in a small voice.

"What?" Zach leans closer to hear me over the wind.

"She might be moving!"

Zach's face morphs from confusion to shock to worry as I tell him everything I know. He thought Operation Candy Empire was just about paying for Science Kidz, but now he gets it.

"I'll help you," he says. "Anything you need."

I know he will, despite everything else he has going on. But how will he help me if Grandma actually moves to Florida?

"How do you handle it?" I ask him. "Every time there's another huge upheaval at your house?"

He's quiet for so long I think maybe the wind drowned my words. But then I see he's got his thoughtful face on. Finally he says, "I guess I always trust that my parents are doing what they believe is right for our whole family. Not easy, but right. It's been true every time so far."

We both watch as the Bainbridge Island ferry dock comes into view across the water.

"But then," he adds, "the upheavals at my house are always about adding a new family member. Not losing one."

Exactly.

11
Pay Attention

We're at the theater an hour before rehearsal starts the next day, because Mom has a production meeting with the designers. Since I can't eavesdrop from the lighting grid anymore, I'm sitting a couple of rows behind them and listening in.

But grid or not, I get to see Ana María in action. She's cosmically awesome.

The old stage manager just sat there during production meetings, doodling in a notebook. (Mom thought he was taking notes, but I could totally see the page from the lighting grid.) The designers would all blab on and on and talk over each other, and they'd go way longer than they were supposed to, and Mom would always have a migraine after.

Ana María is running this meeting like there's a countdown clock and they've got to get through all the business before the whole theater explodes. So far she's said, "Let's keep on track, please?" seven times. She's taking actual notes—I'm sitting where I can see her computer screen—and when someone rambles on too long, she says, "Great, let's follow up about that on email. Moving on."

Mom is even sneaking M&M's from her bag, and she never eats chocolate when a headache is coming on.

The only hiccup is when Mom and Mrs. Freymiller start talking about the costume parade.

"A costume parade?" Ana María interjects. "Is that a good use of rehearsal time?"

The way she says it, though, you can tell she believes it is definitely not a good use of rehearsal time.

Mom looks at her like she has three heads. "Of course it is. We always do costume parades."

"Oh. All right then." Ana María's not going to push the issue, but now Mom is distracted.

"Don't they do costume parades at OSF?"

"No, not at any professional theater I've worked at."

Mom turns to Mrs. Freymiller, who says, "Have you worked at any children's theaters, dear?"

And that's the end of that conversation.

When the meeting's finally over, I know I should be cool. Ana María has been clear about not wanting my help. But I'm overwhelmed by how awesome she was at running that meeting, and how it seemed like she knew everything about the lights, especially, and I really want to impress her.

Unfortunately, what comes out when I block her way up the aisle is, "I can name all the female astronauts in order from Valentina Tereshkova to Jessica Meir."

She looks over her shoulder, like maybe there's someone else behind her who might care.

"You have a NASA sticker!" I blurt.

"Oh. Yeah." She scoots past me to keep walking up the aisle but turns to say something else, so I follow after her, practically running to keep up with her long strides. "I got to meet Mae Jemison once."

"What? No way!"

"Way. She's a friend of my aunt's."

"Oh my shooting stars."

We're almost at the back of the theater. She'll turn to go up to the booth, where I'm not allowed, so I scramble for something else to say. "You also have a roller skates sticker!"

"Yep. Are you into roller-skating, too?"

"Not really."

She looks at me a little funny. "Okay. Well. Excuse me, Zadie."

So it wasn't the most impressive conversation, but it was a conversation that didn't include her telling me no. I'm considering that progress.

Next stop: the universe! (Or at least Ana María teaching me her cosmically awesome ways.)

Once rehearsal is underway, I'm restless. Progress with Ana María means there's hope to actually impress her the next time, which makes sitting around doing nothing even worse. I'm in the wings, because I'd be bored to pieces in the audience, and the wings are the next best thing to the lighting grid, because I can see backstage and onstage, and at least some of the audience, sometimes.

I'm perched on a pile of tumbling mats Mom uses when kids are learning fight choreography, brainstorming ideas for a lunar rover that can travel farther distances, when the loading dock door opens. It's this giant door backstage, like a garage door, where set pieces can be brought in, since big stuff is usually built away from the theater. Sunlight floods through the wings and onto the stage.

Out in the house, I hear Ana María say, "Hold, please!" The kids onstage stop mid-scene. "Did someone open the loading dock door?"

Suddenly I have a purpose! A chance to show how helpful I am! As Fiona the set designer lugs the door open, I dart onto the stage. "It's Fiona!" I report.

"Oh, okay. Actors, take it from, 'She must wed the prince,' please."

The actors go back to their scene, and there I am on the stage, frozen.

"Uh, Zadie? Can you leave the stage?"

The kids giggle, and I scuttle back to the loading dock door.

"Hey, Zadie," Fiona says. "Can you give me a hand?"

Fiona is delivering some set pieces she's going to come back to paint later. Nothing's too heavy, but they're a little awkward to handle, so I help her get them through the door and propped up against the back wall. There are a couple of bushes, and the front of a tower, which Lulu will climb a ladder and stand behind like she's looking through the window. We also lug some paint cans in from Fiona's truck, plus a bucket with a tarp and brushes and one of those trays you pour the paint into.

"Thanks, Zadie, you're the best." Fiona grins and puts her hand up for a high five, but then she winces and grabs at her shoulder.

"You okay?"

"Oh you know, getting too old for building sets. I pulled something last night. Hey, tell your mom and Ana María that I'll be back this evening to paint, if they can leave the alarm off."

"Okay!"

As soon as Fiona has gone, I sneak out into the house to deliver the message to my mom right away, because I'm not going to be the reason the alarm goes off when Fiona returns.

I wander back to the wings, planning to keep brainstorming my lunar rover, but the set pieces and cans of paint are just sitting there. Full of potential. On the hierarchy of theater tech, lighting is obviously the top. Literally, ha. Then sound, which is pretty much all computerized. But sets could be cool too. Especially when you get into, like, helicopters landing on the stage and chandeliers crashing from the ceiling.

At BYT we mostly just have painted foam and plywood, but Fiona does some pretty cool stuff with it. I pry open one of the lids on the paint cans, out of curiosity. Green. And the other one has gray. Obviously green for the bushes and gray for the tower. I've seen Fiona paint sets before. She'll paint the base color, and then go back and do all kinds of cool detail.

I could never do the detail stuff, but a monkey could do the base color painting. And Fiona's shoulder is injured. She'd probably be thrilled to come back and find the base color already done.

Is it something my mom would say I could do if I asked her? Probably not. (Definitely not.) But could I do it before the end of the day, and then impress Ana María by having done it? Probably yes!

I spread the tarp out and lug one of the bushes onto it. I ponder the can of green paint. I consider dipping the brush in the paint can, but there must be a reason real set painters pour it out into the flat pan, and I'm determined to get this right. Basically, I have to do this whole thing like peeing in outer space: very carefully.

The can of paint is heavy, and I slosh more out than I probably need. Some spills over the sides, but that's what the tarp is there for. No worries.

I'm surprised by how satisfying it is to stroke the bright green paint across the bush-shaped plywood. But about forty-five minutes later, I'm still not done with the first bush, and I'm starting to understand why Fiona's shoulder is bothering her. I'm not going to let a little thing like screaming muscles stop me, though. Ana María didn't get to be master electrician (aka Queen of The Grid) at the Oregon Shakespeare Festival without paying some dues. I bet she's painted loads of bushes.

I've finally finished the first one when Ana María announces that it's snack time. For once they didn't ask me to set it up, and not that I'm complaining, but today I actually wanted to! I have a backpack stuffed full of licorice to sell on the sly while handing out graham crackers. Operation Candy Empire is underway, after all.

But Ana María would never leave a tray full of paint out, and snack is twenty minutes, so I have time. I pour the leftover paint from the tray back into the can (mostly), toss the messy brush back into the bucket of supplies, which are all paint-splattered already, then leave the freshly painted bush to dry on the tarp, in case of drips.

I race to the backstage bathroom to clean the paint off my hands, and I'm glad I do, because I somehow have paint on my arms and face and shirt, too.

By the time I reach the lobby (with my shirt on inside out), there are only a couple of minutes left of snack time. Some kids are already heading back into the theater.

"Zach!" I wave him over. "It's time."

He grins, peering into my backpack at the tub of licorice. "On it. I've already greased the wheels."

Right on cue, Daniel, the little freckled kid, comes over. "I heard you have candy."

"A quarter a piece."

He doesn't hesitate, digging in his pockets and coming up with two quarters, probably for the vending machines, which only have water and juice. I hand over his loot.

"Thanks!" he says. "I'm sorry you got kicked out of the cast."

I shrug. "I didn't want to be in it anyway. I'm more of a tech person. But thanks. You're really funny."

Daniel plays the court jester, and he's constantly stealing scenes from Blair and Maddie, which boosts him up several levels, in my opinion.

Zach looks at me funny. "Since when are you 'more of a tech person'? I thought you didn't want anything to do with theater."

"You know, Zachary," I say as I shove a piece of licorice in his mouth to shut him up, "a person is allowed to grow and change."

I use some of the snack napkins to wrap up

more of the candy stash, which I pass to Zach. "Can you get to the kids who've already gone into the theater?"

"Dude, you know there's no food inside."

"That's why I need you. My mom would notice me approaching everyone, but you're like the mayor of BYT."

Flattery will do it every time. Zach holds out his hands. "I'm gonna need more licorice."

While Mayor Zach goes to peddle his goods inside the theater, I work the lobby.

"You guys need something stronger than graham crackers?" I say to a group sitting by the door, playing some trading card game. I check over my shoulder to make sure no adults are around and then fan out my licorice.

Aidan looks up and narrows his eyes. "What do you want for it?"

Freckles didn't bat an eye at a quarter a piece, and this crowd is mostly summer squatters who I know have money.

"I'm only asking a fair price. Covering my costs, you know. Fifty cents a piece."

(I don't tell him that I'm covering the cost

of my licorice and my grandmother's basement apartment. Hopefully.)

Aidan scoffs and turns back to his cards. One of the girls says, "Sorry, I don't carry cash." One tells me licorice has gluten (who knew?), so this is clearly not my crowd.

I scarf a piece of licorice myself, though I'm going to have to be careful not to eat too much of my own inventory. Then I duck into the theater, where I catch Zach's eye, and he gives me a thumbs-up.

"Okay, we're back!" Ana María calls. "We're going to take it from the top of act two. If you're not in the scene, you're sitting in the house. Quietly."

I'm making my way down the aisle to go backstage and paint the second bush, when Blair and Maddie come scurrying out of the wings, where they spent their break plotting world domination or whatever they do.

Oh space junk!

I notice the bright green footprints tromping across the stage a half second before Maddie screams. Ana María is a blur, reaching the stage at the speed of light and immediately issuing an order for everyone to freeze where they are.

Where I am is on the first step up to the stage. If I move, I'll be noticed, without a doubt. But at that moment I want to sink through the stairs into the crawl space under the stage and even farther down into the hot molten core of the earth.

Any second now, Ana María or my mother is going to put together the fact that Fiona arrived and dropped off sets and paint and I was there, because I reported her arrival, and then somehow paint got left out for Blair and Maddie to step in and track across the stage (and all over their shoes, which are apparently very precious and expensive, based on their wails).

But I took the time to put the paint away! That's why I barely had time to sell any candy! The only thing I left out was the tarp. Which had paint spilled on it. Kind of a lot.

Ana María and my mom lock eyes across the theater. Then they both turn on me.

"ZADIE!!!"

12
Take Responsibility

The next morning I can barely get out of bed. Even rolling over hurts.

Not only did I paint the entire bush (which no one thanked me for), but after we had dinner at home, Mom dragged me back to the theater, where she made me paint the entire floor of the stage! By myself!

Fiona was there when we arrived, doing details on the bush I'd painted earlier.

"Thanks for your help, Zadie," she whispered.

Mom heard with her bionic ears and shot Fiona a Look.

Mom helped me clear stuff off the stage and

poured black paint into trays, but then she settled into her regular seat in the audience with a stack of scripts to read.

"Why can't I just paint over the green splotches?" I asked. My shoulder was already getting sore.

"Because then there'll be splotches of fresh, glossy black all over the rest of the dingy, scuffed-up stage! It'll look ridiculous!"

I knew better than to ask for help. I'd lobbied for Papa or Grandma to be the one to bring me back to the theater, because I knew they wouldn't make me do it by myself. Mom knew that too.

I could tell Fiona wanted to help me, but Mom sent her home the second she finished working on the bush.

I do not like to admit this, but at first it was a little bit fun. I got to use this long-handled roller brush, sort of like a broom. I felt like a chimney sweep from *Mary Poppins*. I sang "Step in Time" softly while I danced around the brush. But then I noticed Mom watching me.

"Sorry." I went back to painting dutifully.

"No, don't stop," she said, surprising me. "There's no reason you can't have fun while doing it. I simply don't understand why you won't share your wonderful creativity with an audience."

It wasn't a question, so I didn't answer. I thought about it, though, while I kept painting.

I don't have stage fright (except during auditions, apparently). I can do school reports and talk in front of people with no problem. I don't mind being the center of attention even, like telling a joke in the cafeteria that gets everyone laughing. I think what I don't like is the idea of pretending to be someone else.

Why waste time pretending, when there are so many real things in the universe that haven't even been discovered yet?

But this morning there is nothing in the universe that can make it more fun to be me. Mom eventually broke down and helped me finish, but we still didn't get home until nearly midnight. Every muscle in my body is screaming when Papa pokes his head into our room.

"Up and at 'em, mija!"

I don't bother looking to see if Lulu is already up. Of course she is, and I don't have enough energy to move my eyeballs.

"Can I stay home today?"

"Nope, I'm not going to be home."

"I can stay home alone."

Papa opens the door all the way and leans against the doorframe. "I don't think so. You managed to vandalize the stage while the theater was full of people. What would happen to the house if we left you here alone?"

I haul my body up to sitting. "I didn't vandalize the stage!"

"I know." Papa sighs. "I wish you could come with me, but it's my first day driving. Ryde drivers aren't supposed to have family members tagging along, and I need my reviews to be good."

Ugh. As much as I hate my own life right now, I hate Papa's even more. He's this amazing musician who can play more instruments than I can keep track of, but he has to worry about what strangers think of his driving.

So I manage to get myself out of bed and down the stairs. I don't change out of pajamas and don't even care. I don't eat breakfast, because chewing is hard work. I'm fast asleep, drooling with my face plastered to the window, when the car stops at the theater.

"We're here, Spinderella," Lulu says, poking me.

Very funny. Spinderella. Because she falls into an enchanted sleep. I would kill for a magical spindle to knock me out until this show is over.

I get through another week without disaster. Unless you count the death of most of my brain cells from complete and utter boredom. Ana María continues to look at me like I am a cockroach worthy of being dumped in her least favorite kid's backpack, and I'm too afraid for a repeat of the paint disaster to take much initiative around the theater.

I get a few faithful candy customers—Daniel may rival Zach for sugar obsession—but by the end of the week, I have to face facts. Operation Candy Empire might be a mission failure.

Too many kids don't carry cash, or else they bring their own good snacks or run to the fancy market before rehearsals officially start. Grandma's excitement over my profit margins only worked if I sold out of everything, and I am nowhere near close to the stated goals of the mission.

Which means I'm nowhere near keeping Grandma here, where she belongs.

This must be what NASA engineers felt like when they had to shut down the shuttle program.

By the time Monday comes around again, I think Mom has forgiven me for the paint incident (though she definitely has not forgotten). When Mrs. Freymiller arrives mid-rehearsal with her arms full, Mom sends me to help her carry stuff to the dressing rooms.

"Ah, Zadie, my little costume assistant!" Mrs. Freymiller crows, her fiery red scarf trailing after her like flames from a rocket as we carry boxes down the stairs behind the stage. "How are you?"

"I'm okay," I say. "Your daughter had a baby, right? Congratulations."

"She did! Thank you! Little Petronella Constantina Freymiller-Rubenstein is the most perfect baby to ever grace this earth!"

I'm sort of glad the hallway down here is dark so she doesn't see my face. I thought it was tough to find personalized stuff with the name Zadie on it. Little Petronella Constantina is going to have a rough childhood.

But she'll have Mrs. Freymiller for a grandma, and a good grandma makes up for a lot. It helps if she lives nearby, though. Right downstairs is ideal. Especially if that grandma is the only one in her whole entire family who gets her at all, or even if she doesn't exactly get her, she at least lets her be who she is without making her feel like she's as alien as a microorganism growing on the outside of the International Space Station.

In the dressing rooms, Mrs. Freymiller unpacks costumes and hangs them on racks for tomorrow's costume parade. Costume parades are a thing I've known about since I was toddling around the theater in diapers, like the ghost light we always keep on even when we go home, or not saying "Macbeth" inside the theater, or how when you give away a bunch of tickets so it seems like the show is full and selling really well, it's called "papering the house."

But the first time Zach heard we were doing a costume parade, he thought there would be floats and confetti and giant balloon animals.

(To be fair, we were only like six.) It turns out costume parades are just when the actors try on the costumes and show them to the director and designer, and the director says, "Oh, I think she might trip on that hem in the ball scene. Can you bring it up a little?"

It's really pretty boring.

And apparently, according to Ana María, they don't even do them in professional theaters anymore. But Mom and Mrs. Freymiller are old school, plus they know what works at BYT.

Even if costume parades are old hat for me, watching the costumes emerge from their garment bags for the first time is definitely exciting. Mrs. Freymiller lets me unbox the wigs and arrange them on their Styrofoam heads along the counter in the dressing room.

Lulu gets a super-dramatic wig with masses of curly red hair. Amaya, who plays Spinderella herself, has a long, chestnut-brown braid that'll hang dramatically down the side of the bed where she sleeps. Blair and Maddie have these super-fancy hairstyles all covered in white-blond braids and curls, perfect for the two queens.

"You like the wigs?" Mrs. Freymiller says as she hangs the last costumes on the rack. "You can try them on, if you want."

I imagine Ana María's face if she came down and found me trying on the wigs. "That's okay."

"Suit yourself. But if you'd like to help, they could use a brushing before the costume parade."

Costumes are a long distance from the lighting grid. But one of the designers is giving me clear directions on how to help. Success will mean points in Ana María's book. (It's more of a giant binder, where she keeps every single scrap of information about the show, but it's basically a book, and I'm convinced she's keeping a running tally of my failures.)

She sets a hairbrush on the counter. "You can't mess up brushing a wig. It would be a big help to me. I'll tell your mom, okay?"

"Okay." She gathers the empty boxes and garment bags and piles them in a corner. "If you ever want to learn more about costume design, you know who to ask, Miss Zadie."

Next step: getting Ana María to feel the same way.

I pounce on the brush before her sparkly purple shoes hit the first step. "Thank you, Mrs. Freymiller!"

She waves her manicured hand over her shoulder as she disappears up the stairs. "Au revoir, Zadie!"

I start with Lulu's wig. The hair is so tangled and curly that the brush won't go through it. But I don't force it. I definitely don't want to damage it, and Grizelda's hair shouldn't be smooth and silky. Straight out of the box rumpled is honestly perfect.

To make sure, I decide to try it on. Mrs. Freymiller did say I could, after all. But putting on a wig isn't as easy as you'd think. Taming my own bushy hair into a ponytail is the first step. I've seen Lulu do this before. She puts this sort of pantyhose cap on her head to flatten things out, but I don't have one handy, and it's not like I need to convince an audience that it's my real hair.

Once my own hair is under control, I take the Grizelda wig from its Styrofoam head. I try to tug it on, like putting on a hat, but at first it's way too far forward on my face, and then when I tug it back, you can see like three inches of my own hair. Finally I get it settled pretty well and look in the mirror.

Okay, maybe I have to ignore my own brown hair sticking out along the hairline, but still! Wow! I look like a total evil villain, ready to take down a nemesis!

I turn to Blair's and Maddie's wigs, because they're the closest things I've got to a nemesis. Nemeses? Does the plural of "nemesis" ever come up, or by definition does a hero only have one supreme nemesis? Whatever, they can be combined into one. Mair. No, Bladdie.

Even if Bladdie is my nemesis, I'm going to do right by their wigs. That way when their performances are spectacular failures, it will be completely due to their lack of talent. (They actually have decent talent, but letting myself think about that opens a whole can of worms about why good things happen to bad people and how bad people can make good things, and Grizelda doesn't think about things that deeply. She's black and white, and so am I right now.)

I spend forever on their wigs, making sure every curl shines and hangs in the perfect position.

There's not much to do with Spinderella's wig, since it's already in a braid, but I smooth out the top part and brush the fluffy little pouf at the end.

They look amazing. But I know what the dressing room will be like tomorrow when the cast descends to try on costumes for the parade. There will be dozens of kids down here, everyone with their own water bottles and snacks they're not supposed to have, jostling for only a few outlets to charge the devices they're also not supposed to have. These wigs are going to get bumped around.

Grizelda's wig is supposed to be a total mess, so that's no problem, and Spinderella's is just a long braid. But the hairstyles of the two queens are super intricate. They require extra protection.

What I need is hair spray. It doesn't take any special skills to spray hair spray, so I'm feeling confident. And it doesn't take me long to find some either. Even though Mom tries to bribe the casts to clean up after shows close, the dressing room never gets completely clean. That's why I can already spot from where I'm standing prosthetic beaver teeth from *The Lion, the Witch and the Wardrobe* (when I was eight), a pot of green face paint from *The Wizard of Oz* (when I was four), and a lone tap shoe that could be from a whole bunch of different shows.

With the can of hair spray in hand, I hold my breath and spray the wigs, careful to cover them evenly so the work I've done won't be wasted when the crowds descend.

Perfect. No one can deny I've helped today.

I'm in the lobby, setting out the snack without even being asked, when Ana María bursts in from the theater, my mom hurrying after her.

"What on earth is this?!"

She thrusts one of the queen wigs (weirdly threatening on its Styrofoam head) into my face. It still looks fantastic, so clearly the hair spray worked.

"That's Queen Lavinia's wig. Mrs. Freymiller dropped it off. The others are here too."

"Oh, I know."

She's vibrating with rage, like Valentina Tereshkova must have been when the Russian space agency blamed her for a programming error that was totally not her fault. I still don't see the problem.

"I brushed them," I admit. "But Mrs. Freymiller asked me to. You can ask her!"

"You brushed them!" She turns to Mom, sputtering. I realize now that Mom is holding Queen Brunhilda's wig, looking miserable. Ana María violently shakes Queen Lavinia's head. The kids have started trailing out of the theater and gather round to watch the spectacle.

"Is that my wig?" Blair shrieks, her voice going up to a dangerous decibel.

I look from her horrified face back to the poor abused wig, and that's when I realize that it's not moving. Not a hair. Ana María is violently shaking the Styrofoam head, but the wig moves with it like it's all one solid piece. A helmet. For the big finish, Ana María turns the head over, and the wig falls off, clunking to the floor, completely intact.

"What did you do?" Blair lunges forward, like I've run over her puppy.

Mom turns to the group of rubbernecking kids. "Okay, everyone back in the theater."

"But it's snack time," Aidan whines.

"We'll get to it. Give us a minute." She zeroes in on Zach. "Zach? Lead some improv games?"

Zach throws me a sympathetic look before heading back into the theater. Most of the kids reluctantly follow him. But Blair and Maddie stay, and Aidan lingers in the doorway.

"Zadie Louise." Mom sets Queen Brunhilda's head on the snack table. I reach out and poke it. My finger can't move a single hair; it's basically a sculpture. "You didn't only brush them."

"She did this on purpose!" Maddie wails. "She has it out for us!"

Mom takes a deep breath and focuses on me. "What happened?"

"I brushed them," I insist. "And I might have used some hair spray. That's all."

Ana María reaches into the OSF bag over her shoulder. She pulls out the can of hair spray. "With this?"

My heart sinks as I look at the label. Oh turbo-charged space junk. INDUSTRIAL-STRENGTH SPRAY ADHESIVE. Under the alarming orange letters, it says, *For a permanent, unbreakable bond!*

I sprayed the wigs with glue.

"These wigs are completely ruined," Ana María says, her voice no longer hysterical. Now it's plain deadly. "I don't even know what to say."

"I thought it was hair spray." I hate how my voice trembles. I hate even more that Blair and Maddie and Aidan are all watching this happen. "It was an accident."

"Then why is it only our wigs?" Blair demands. "Why not Lulu's or Amaya's?"

Mom and Ana María both look at me. This is bad. And there's no way I can explain with them all looking at me like I've been plotting to take over a planet for its rich mineral reserves.

"I just, I can't." Ana María turns to Mom, like I'm not even worth talking to. "I should have known children's theater wasn't going to be a fit for me."

"Ana María." Mom's eyes dart to the other cast members listening in.

"No, it's beyond ridiculous that I have to put up with her sabotage, on top of everything else!"

"Ana María." Mom's tone is sharper now, like when she's caught me reading comic books instead of doing math. "We'll discuss this after rehearsal. For now, you don't need to worry about Zadie."

Ana María meets Mom's gaze but finally turns and stalks to the lobby bathroom. At a withering glare from Mom, Blair, Maddie, and Aidan head back into the theater.

"Mom." My chin wobbles. "It really was an accident."

She sighs. "I know. But the damage is still done."

Grandma Sooz pulls up in front of the theater twenty minutes later. "Hop in!" she calls from the car. I've been sitting in the drizzle on the half wall outside since Mom banished me. "I've only got ten minutes before my next class starts!"

Pretty soon Grandma won't be able to swoop to the rescue every time Mom needs to get rid of me. I should try to enjoy any time with her I can get, but that's pretty much impossible, considering I can't shake off the sick feeling of everyone looking at me like I'm the worst kind of space junk.

She tosses an extra hand towel at me as I

climb in. I don't even care that water's dripping down my face, but I guess there's no reason to take this horrible day out on Grandma's upholstery, so I try to dry off. Then I stare at the logo on the towel—three intertwined Zs for Zoom Zoom Zumba. Or Zig-Zag Zadie. The tears in my eyes blur the Zs into a meaningless tangle.

That's what all this is. I could handle losing my favorite activities, by itself. I could handle everyone thinking I've done something horrible, if that's all I had going on. I could maybe possibly even handle Grandma needing to move out of our house if everyone would just be honest and clear about it. Make a plan about how often she'll visit us and we'll visit her and . . . I don't know.

Maybe I couldn't handle that one.

But I don't even get the chance to try because it's not just one thing. It's all these things, all tangled up at once.

I follow Grandma inside the Zumba studio and give a half-hearted wave to Ione, the receptionist. She's so old she can barely walk anymore, but she still makes it in to work most days. I'm not sure Grandma even needs her, but Zoom

Zoom Zumba is kind of a home for strays, and she'd never turn anyone away.

Case in point: Martin, sitting in the lobby in his wheelchair. He used to do classes in his chair and just do the arm movements, but lately his joints won't let him do even that much. So he comes to the studio and hangs out, chatting with everyone as they come and go.

"Hi, Zelda!" Martin has always called me by a different Z-name every time he sees me. It started as a joke, but now I'm pretty sure he doesn't remember my actual name. And it's pretty impressive how many Z-names he's come up with. I've had a much easier time coming up with M-names for him.

"Hi, Maxwell," I manage, as I settle onto the comfiest couch in the lobby.

"Sure you don't want to join us for the class?" Grandma calls to me on her way in to the big, mirror-lined room.

"Maybe later."

She winks. She knows I won't accept, but she never stops offering. It's not that it doesn't look fun. It actually looks super fun, with the catchy music and Grandma cracking jokes the whole

113

time. Sometimes Lulu does a class, and the old people fawn all over her, like she's the greatest gift to Zumba the world has ever known. But that's Lulu, happy in the spotlight.

When Grandma moves, I won't only be losing her. I'll be losing Zoom Zoom Zumba. Even if I don't take the classes, I've been hanging out here since Grandma started the studio when I was in preschool. It's a second home, way more comfortable than the theater. But a new owner isn't going to be cool with some random kid hanging around. And I wouldn't want to anyway, not without Grandma Sooz.

I pull a comic book from my bag, but I can't focus on it. And it's not only because Martin is having a rousing conversation with a tiny lady I haven't seen before about all their friends who've died or are about to die.

Everyone thinks I destroyed the wigs on purpose, but they also think I specifically sabotaged Blair's and Maddie's wigs. That's the kind of thing they would do! But even worse, it sounds like Ana María is miserable at Bainbridge Youth Theater and it's all my fault!

I guess I can't blame her. She was the master electrician at the Oregon Shakespeare Festival! And now she's cleaning up my messes at a dinky kids' theater on a remote island. That's like if Valentina Tereshkova could only fly stomp rockets!

One class ends and another begins. Martin goes in to watch the next class, I think because he has a crush on Matilde, who has fire-engine red hair and always wears lipstick to match.

Toward the end of the second class, I see a woman approaching the entrance with a walker, so I jump up to open the door for her.

"Thank you, dear." She makes her way over to check in at the front desk. "You have an assistant today, I see," she tells Ione.

Ione beams at me, like I've done anything to help her for two hours. I should have offered to sweep or something. But I'd probably mess that up too.

"Do you know Zadie?" Ione asks the woman. "She's Sooz's granddaughter!"

"Oh, lovely! Aren't grandchildren wonderful?" Ione's face falls. She has one daughter who never married. But the woman doesn't seem to notice.

"Do you know Oscar Gutierrez? His granddaughter left a fancy show business job to come home and take care of him. All for nothing, if you ask me. He'll go into a nursing home sooner rather than later."

Ione shakes her head.

I think of the retirement home in Florida where Grandma Sooz might go. Maybe those people need her and the happiness she would bring them. But what about my happiness?

"Show business?" Ione says. "You mean like Hollywood?"

"No, *theater*!" She pronounces it in this fancy way, like theater is super glamorous. (It's not.) "Poor thing is stuck working with the children's theater now."

The children's theater. There's only one children's theater on Bainbridge Island. Ione glances at me; she knows who my mom is, but this other lady clearly doesn't. Ione changes the subject, but I am left with what this woman has said.

Oscar Gutierrez. He must be Ana María's

grandfather. She had to leave Oregon and come here because he needs her. But even after that sacrifice, she might lose him to a nursing home.

Ana María and I have more in common than I thought.

13
Follow Direction

I drag my heels getting to the car the next morning. Who can blame me?

(My mom.)

(And Lulu.)

They're not blaming me for the wigs at least. Mom's lecture last night was totally half-hearted since this time it seems she understood it was an accident. But Ana María got so mad at me yesterday. And everyone else thinks I sabotaged Blair's and Maddie's wigs. And oh space junk—I don't even think of it until I'm buckling into the car—Mrs. Freymiller is going to be so disappointed in me. She actually trusted me with something important, and I managed to screw it up!

"It's going to be fine," Mom says as she stops in the drive-through coffee place right past Frog Rock. "It's costume parade day. Everyone will be busy, and you can help people zip up costumes and make sure their crowns are straight."

"Just don't glue the crowns to their heads," Lulu says.

"Lourdes."

"Sorry."

I don't kick the back of the passenger seat, because I'm actually relieved to hear Lulu make a snarky comment. She's been freakishly nice to me since yesterday. But it's because she believes I sabotaged Blair's and Maddie's wigs too. At least, I think so.

Mom eyes me in the rearview mirror as she waits for her coffee. "I know you're still noodling on what Ana María said yesterday, but I don't want you to worry. She was out of line, talking like that in front of you. She's going through a lot, and we're going to give her some grace. Like we do for each other."

I know now what Ana María's going through, but I'm keeping my mouth shut. I can't add spilling secrets to my list of reasons for her to hate me.

No, I'm staying focused today. I thought about stuffing my backpack with candy and trying to restart Operation Candy Empire. Lots of people will be in and out of the dressing rooms with no adult supervision, waiting around for their turn to show their costume to Mom and Mrs. Freymiller. But the whole week I tried selling candy, I only made $9.25. It's just not worth it when I need to lie low.

When we reach the theater, I zip through the lobby with my head down, trying my best to ignore Bladdie's glares.

"I was so excited for costume parade!" I can't help hearing Maddie as I pass through. "But now my wig is ruined!"

"Hey, Zadie, where's the fire?" Zach jogs to catch up with me as I rush through the theater.

"You shouldn't say 'fire' in a crowded theater."

Zach looks around. There are only a couple of kids inside at the moment. "Look, no one really believes you messed up the wigs on purpose. Or if they do, they only wish they'd done it themselves."

I muster half a smile and dig out some licorice I brought just for him. "Thanks, Zach."

He takes it but grabs my arm as I start to go. "Hey, thanks. But I didn't say that for candy, you know."

"I know."

"You have somewhere to be? Or do you want to hang in the dressing room during costume parade?"

I don't really want to hang around with the whole cast and deal with whispers and questions about the wigs. But on the other hand, Zach is one of the only people on my side. I follow him to the dressing room, which is empty for now.

I've barely set down my backpack when I hear Mrs. Freymiller's voice coming down the stairs.

"Oh, Marinee, it's fine!" She's talking to my mom.

I drag Zach behind the folding screen that blocks off the corner where the boys change their clothes.

"These things happen," Mrs. Freymiller goes on. "Do you think I haven't seen worse?"

"I know, I just want you to know she didn't do it intentionally. Zadie isn't like that."

"Of course she isn't. I know that."

My heart swells a little. Up until that moment I hadn't realized it, but I thought maybe my mom was only saying she believed me to calm me down. It's a huge relief to know she really does. And so does Mrs. Freymiller.

"She gets carried away, you know? Doesn't think things through. It's one disaster after another."

Oof. My heart deflates like a punctured space suit. I avoid Zach's eyes, not able to bear seeing pity there.

"Oh, honey, I seem to remember another young woman who was eager to stick her nose in every area of the theater, even when she wasn't the most qualified."

Mom lets out a sharp laugh. "Oh, well, you've got me there, Vivienne!"

They head for the stairs, done with whatever they were doing in the dressing rooms. "Do you remember that time," Mrs. Freymiller says, "that all of the angel costumes got dyed hot pink?"

"I'd call it more of a bubblegum pink. . . ."

I'm dying to hear the rest of that story, but they're gone now. And I can't ask Mom later or she'll know I was eavesdropping. I might be able to get it out of Mrs. Freymiller, though.

"See," Zach says as we step out from behind the screen. "Everyone knows it was an accident."

I wish I had a folding screen to enclose myself as kids start to trickle into the dressing room. I settle for the corner with the least traffic and keep my head down while Ana María and Mrs. Freymiller give the kids instructions. Then, like I knew they would, the adults head up to the house while the kids are left to get their costumes on.

Instead of coming up and down the stairs, Ana María calls for whoever's next from the top, and they head up to walk across the stage and let Mom and Mrs. Freymiller get a good view of the costume. They'll consult together on whether or not it needs any changes, and then that kid is released to come down and get into their next costume. Or, if they only have the one costume, they're released to goof off in the dressing room for the rest of costume parade.

Zach stays with me, instead of bonding with his castmates like he normally would. I feel selfish, not telling him to go hang out with them. But it helps, having him here. Zach's like my family, loving the spotlight, loving to pretend. But he's also like me because he's the only one of his kind in his family. I don't mean because of his appearance—his dads and siblings have a whole range of skin colors, eye colors, and hair types— but no one in his family gets the theater thing. Jacob's a math teacher, and Jim's a city planner. Micah, Jasmine, and Namina all play sports; the twins are too little to say.

Zach fits right in with my family. But I don't fit with his any more than I fit with mine. I don't care about sports. Chasing a ball, chasing a spotlight. Doesn't anyone else want to chase the stars? See what's out there besides what we're stuck with here?

I'm helping Zach run his lines when Lulu comes over to us, her face red. As she gets close enough, I realize she's fighting tears.

"What's wrong?" I scoot over so she can sit next to me. But she doesn't.

"What's wrong is my costume doesn't fit!"

I look from her face to the beautiful black

gown she's wearing. The fabric is shimmery and the edges are ragged, but like, artfully ragged. There's amazing embroidery all over the bodice. Mrs. Freymiller's outdone herself.

"It looks fine to me."

Lulu whirls around to show me the wide-open zipper, about four inches away from closing. There's no corset in the world that could close that thing.

"This is your fault," she spits out as the tears spill over. "You're coming with me to explain this to Mom."

"How is this my fault?"

She grabs my arm and drags me to the stairs. Everybody's watching and whispering, and Blair and Maddie are gleeful. Which makes no sense, because their whole argument that I'd sabotaged their wigs was based on the idea that I didn't sabotage my own sister's costume.

"I'm sure Mrs. Freymiller can fix it!" I cry, grabbing onto the handrail so I don't trip as she yanks me up the stairs.

At the top, Ana María frowns. "They're not ready for you, Lulu."

My sister pushes past her with me in tow. I look helplessly back at Ana María, which is a mistake because then I see the horror on her face when she realizes why Lulu is so upset.

"Mom!" Lulu wails.

A pair of townspeople who were getting their costumes assessed at center stage shrink to the side as Lulu gets her spotlight. (Not really. There's no spot operator right now.)

"Zadie? Lulu, what on earth—"

Lulu whirls around dramatically, letting the way-too-small costume speak for itself.

Mrs. Freymiller lets out a yelp. Mom sighs.

"It's all Zadie's fault!" Lulu announces as both Mom and Mrs. Freymiller rush for the stage, like she has a lethal tear in her Extravehicular Mobility Unit and not an ill-fitting costume.

"How is it Zadie's fault?" Mom asks.

"She took the measurements!"

Mrs. Freymiller worries her tape measure between ruby red-tipped fingers and frets over the dress. No one looks me in the eye.

"That might explain some of the other fit issues," Ana María offers.

There've been other fit issues?

"To be fair," Ana María goes on. "That was probably too difficult a task to trust to her."

I don't know whether I should be insulted or grateful she's (sort of) sticking up for me.

"I did exactly what I was told! I measured people with the tape and wrote it down in the right place. I was so careful! I even learned what an armscye is!"

"I knew it was a mistake to trust you," Lulu sobs.

Ana María retrieves her magical binder and flips to the page with Lulu's measurements. "This says her waist is twenty-eight inches."

Mom and Mrs. Freymiller exchange a glance I can't quite decipher.

"Look! I'll show you!" I take the tape measure from Mrs. Freymiller's hands and do exactly what I did before. I hold the tape measure at one end, carefully wrap it around Lulu's waist, making sure it lies flat and doesn't twist, and then join the end of the tape to the rest.

It clearly stops at twenty-eight inches. I am vindicated.

Mom was so quick to blame me, but now she looks relieved. Maybe I'm not such a disaster.

But Mrs. Freymiller's face is a different story. "Oh dear." She takes the tape measure from my hands, holding it in the same spots. "You measured from the wrong end."

Huh?

She holds it out so we can see. Sure enough, one end is on twenty-eight inches. But instead of holding the other end at the zero, she's holding it at the sixty-inch mark.

Mom's not a numbers person, so she's still confused. But Ana María gets it. "It looks like twenty-eight inches," she says. "But twenty-eight inches away from sixty is actually thirty-two inches. So the measurement Zadie wrote down is four inches too small."

Mom buries her head in her hands for a second. Then she pops back up. "All right. Moving forward, what can be done? Can this be altered, Viv?"

Mrs. Freymiller bites her fuchsia lip. "I'm afraid not. I used a large portion of the budget on this fabric, and bought only what I needed, according to the measurements. There's no seam allowance to let it out, and even if I had more fabric, all the embroidery next to the seams would be impossible to redo in time. I think we may have to go with something . . . simpler. Perhaps the Wicked Witch costume from *Oz*?"

This is more than Lulu can bear to hear, and she runs from the stage.

I stay. Like it or not (not), I have to know how much I've messed up this time.

Thankfully a lot of the fit issues are easy to fix. It turns out an eight-year-old is not always a size eight (who knew?). But most of the costumes are just stock pieces that got pulled from the costume closet. A villager in *Spinderella* is pretty much the same as a villager in *Beauty and the Beast*, so we can just find costumes in the right sizes for the ones that don't fit. It's the custom pieces that Mrs. Freymiller built from scratch that have had fit issues.

Eventually Mrs. Freymiller needs to get some air and leaves without saying a word to me.

"Oh, Zadie." Mom shakes her head. Then, before walking away, she says pointedly to

Ana María, "And that's why we have a costume parade."

Ana María shuts her giant binder with a thud. "Your mom's been doing this for twenty years and even she didn't realize the problem."

I try to process what she's said.

"Costume design is complex. It's every bit as complex as lights and sound. Drafting patterns is all math. Building costumes is engineering. They wouldn't have asked you to hang and focus the lights all by yourself, and they shouldn't have asked you to do this. Not because you're not trustworthy. Just because you're not experienced.

"This one isn't your fault."

Lulu doesn't speak to me all the way home. Once we're there, she goes into our room and slams the door. I don't blame her for being mad. Her amazing costume was ruined, and no matter what Ana María said, it was my fault.

Even when I'm trying to help, I'm messing things up.

I wander out to the back porch and sit on the steps. Hopefully if I sit here, not doing anything or talking to anyone, I'll avoid causing a disaster for a few minutes, at least. I consider the trees surrounding our house. I've never been a big tree climber, which is weird considering how much I like to be high up in the theater. But we mostly have evergreens around here, and they're not the best for climbing. Imagine trying to climb a Christmas tree.

Still, I might have to figure out tree climbing, so I can climb up high and stay out of everyone's way. It's probably the only way to keep from screwing everything up.

Sir Andrew Lloyd Webber approaches, mrowling at me like I'm going to give him dinner. Ha! I'd rather be Blair's personal assistant for the day than serve that goopy, stinky cat food. But I give him pets. I can't screw up pets. And even if I do, he won't say so.

"I'm sorry you had such a rough day," I hear Papa say, but when I look around, I don't see him. Turns out he's not talking to me. His and Mom's voices both float out the open kitchen window I'm sitting beneath, along with the sounds of their dinner preparations.

"It's always a wild ride, but this show feels cursed," Mom says.

"I understand why Lulu's so upset. The costume sounds like it was really special. But in the grand scheme of things . . ."

"I know it's 'just a play,' but—"

"Your words, not mine! I believe in what you do. Wholeheartedly. You know that. But won't the kids learn just as much and have as much fun in simple costumes as high fashion?"

Point to Papa! All Mom's speeches about arts education are about teamwork and communication skills and self-confidence. You don't need expensive fabric or fancy embroidery for any of those things.

(I mean, astronauts do require pretty specific space suits that protect them from radiation, debris, and extreme temperatures. But it's not like the stage is an inhospitable atmosphere. At least, not to most kids.)

"It's not really about the kids," Mom says. She sounds miserable. "I mean, it is. Of course it is, in the long run. But for right now? It's about funding."

Wait, what?

I listen in horror as she explains to Papa that the arts funding from the island council is on the line. Arts funding that pays her salary and gives our family health insurance. Plus it keeps the theater open. Without the island council's confidence in what Bainbridge Youth Theater offers, all the kids who love BYT as much as I love tae kwon do and Science Kidz could lose it! And they're making their decision right after *Spinderella*'s opening night.

"You really think the island council will be swayed by elaborate costumes?"

"Unfortunately, yes. They don't hear the stories of the painfully shy kid who comes out of their shell on stage. Or the kid with anger management issues who avoids getting sent to juvie because theater gives her a place to channel her feelings. They see what's on the surface. A show that seems like a totally rinky-dink production won't be valuable to them. Eileen learned that the hard way with the bell choir."

I wince, remembering the bell choir "concert" we attended in support of Mom's music-education friend Eileen. I had a headache for three days. But Eileen said the kids were having a marvelous time and that was all that mattered. (Didn't keep the bell choir from being defunded.)

"No show you're in charge of would ever seem . . . rinky-dink? Is that a thing?"

Mom laughs a little. "You have to say that."

"No, I don't. No one's making me. I get that this is serious. The last thing we need right now is for you to lose your job. But I believe in you. And those kids. We'll figure it out."

All my mistakes, they haven't been harmless. They've been adding weight to Mom's shoulders, and threatening not only her job, but the entire theater's existence!

I have to do something. And that something . . . is nothing.

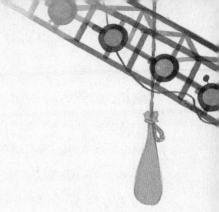

14
Don't Steal Focus

I lay so low for the next week I might as well be carpet.

I will not get in the way. I will not mess things up. I'm dying to be helpful, but the last several times I've tried, I've made everything worse. Not anymore.

I sit and read. I do the boring things I'm asked to do, like setting out snack and folding programs and taping show posters up in all the windows.

I'm slipping Zach his gummy candies at the end of snack time—he hasn't had too much to report about Blair and Maddie besides snarky comments, so mostly I'm giving him candy because he's my best friend (and also I have a ton left over from my failed operation)—when Ana María comes hustling through the lobby, phone to her ear, brow furrowed. We watch her push out the doors to pace on the sidewalk, having some kind of heated discussion with whatever poor soul is on the other end of that phone line.

"Yikes," Zach says. "She looks like my dad when Papa invited his entire soccer team over and they ate all the macarons Dad had made for his boss's birthday."

"She's been taking phone calls all week." I don't mean to be a creeper, but when I'm trying to stay out of the way and sit quietly, I notice stuff. And I've noticed Ana María leaving rehearsals for phone calls and texting furiously even when she's in rehearsal. It's so different from her ultra-professional exterior of the first few weeks. And I'm shocked my mom hasn't called her out for it yet, or at least complained about it at home.

But maybe she doesn't complain because Ana María is still getting everything done. She'll be texting furiously, but if an actor calls for a line, she somehow knows exactly where they're at in a scene and she supplies the line. She seems distracted, but every time Mom has a question, she knows the answer.

And now she's juggling the designers and their needs too, since tech starts this weekend. When we got here this morning, Ana María was up on the lighting grid with Parmida, the new lighting designer. During morning break, she was helping Fiona bring more set pieces in from the loading dock. And for all I know, now she's on the phone with Mrs. Freymiller trying to come up with a solution to Lulu's ruined costume.

Except I don't think so. This looks personal.

And it sounds personal. Right after Zach goes back into rehearsal and I'm left alone to clean up the snack mess in the lobby, the pest control guy arrives. Ana María opens the door for him and waves toward the lobby bathroom. Then before the door swings closed, I hear her say, "Okay, but, Tía, you're not the one here with him. I'm not trying to make you feel guilty—" and then the door swings closed again.

The pest control guy looks at me. "I'm here to fumigate a bathroom?"

I show him where he's supposed to be, then run in to check with my mom and make sure he's in the right place. I'm not going to be responsible for fumigating the wrong room.

"Yes, the lobby bathroom," Mom whispers, as onstage Lulu lets out a spectacular cackle. "Where's Ana María?"

"She's outside. On the phone."

Mom sighs. But she's not irritated. More like sad. "Okay, let me know if the pest guy needs anything, would you, sweetie?"

I nod. I kind of want to stay to watch Lulu's big scene, but I still need to clean up the lobby, and now I need to be there for the pest guy. "Okay."

Mom grabs my hand before I go. "Thanks, Z. I know this isn't the summer of your dreams. But I'm really glad to have you around. When the show's over, maybe you and I can do something special together." She gives my hand an extra squeeze and then turns her attention back to the stage.

I can't remember the last time Mom and I did something special together. I wonder if she means just, like, going out for frozen yogurt. Or if she might mean something like taking the ferry into Seattle for a day at the Pacific Science Center. I wonder if it'll really happen. Usually by the time one show ends, she's prepping for the next one.

That might not happen if the theater doesn't get the funding. But then she'll be even more stressed, desperately looking for a new job. Plus when Grandma moves out, she's going to have to get the basement ready for a renter and find someone to live there.

As I head back into the lobby, Ana María rushes past me into the theater. "Thanks for your help, Zadie," she says.

Whoa. I tell you what: all this appreciation might go to my head!

The pest guy finishes with the lobby bathroom right at the same time I finish picking up the snack mess.

"Hey," I say. "Thanks. Should I get someone to pay you or something?"

"Nah." He holds out a clipboard. "Just sign here."

I blink at him. "I'm ten."

He blinks back. "Can you sign your name?"

I'm not responsible for whatever's happening in that bathroom. Mom and Ana María both know he's here and what he's been doing in there.

I'm only dealing with him so they don't have to. I sign my name.

"Just don't let anyone go in there for the rest of the day, okay?"

"Got it."

I go into the box office (which is not so much an office as a cramped little booth with a window out to the street) and find some old flyers for *The Sound of Music*. On the back, I write, *DANGER! DO NOT ENTER! THIS BATHROOM IS FILLED WITH PESTICIDES! ALL WHO ENTER HERE RISK MUTILATION AND/OR EXTREMELY PAINFUL DEATH.*

Then I draw my best skull and crossbones, which, if I'm honest, look more like a clown on top of some bowling pins (and not even a scary clown). Whatever. I tape the sign onto the bathroom door.

All this thinking about the bathroom (plus probably the three juice boxes I drank while serving snack) have me actually needing a bathroom, and I'm obviously not going to risk mutilation and/or painful death. But that means I have to risk interrupting rehearsal to get backstage.

It's that or go across the street to the coffee shop, and I think I know which one I'll get in more trouble for.

I creep down the aisle. There's a sensitive, emotional scene going on, with Blair as Queen Brunhilda weeping over her daughter's perma-sleeping body, begging her to wake up before the ball.

I especially don't want to interrupt one of Blair's scenes, what with everyone thinking I'm trying to sabotage her, but the apple juice is getting pretty pushy with my bladder. Hopefully Blair is a focused enough actor that she won't notice me climbing up the stairs on the side of the stage. . . .

"Hold, please," Ana María's voice rings out as I'm halfway up. That horrible feeling from the auditions crawls up my spine: all eyes on me, and not for a good reason.

"Zadie?" Mom says in her most irritated tone. "What on earth?"

Everyone is looking at me. I point backstage and mouth, *bathroom*, like that will explain why I'm interrupting.

"Excuse me?"

Ugh. As much as I don't want to, I have no

option but to announce to everyone, "I have to go to the bathroom."

As expected, a couple of kids snicker. I mean, everyone goes to the bathroom, but no one wants to announce it to a room full of people.

Ana María leans over and says something to Mom, who nods. "Fine, go. Don't interrupt again."

I'm almost positive Ana María said, "Pest control." Was she sticking up for me? Explaining to Mom how I would risk mutilation and/or painful death by using the lobby bathroom? In case she was, I give her a grin and a thumbs-up before scurrying backstage.

When I'm done in the bathroom, I hover backstage for a while, since I'm obviously not going to interrupt rehearsal again by slipping down the stairs.

"What are you doing back here?" Maddie hisses in my ear, and I jump, grabbing onto the heavy black velvet curtain so hard it shakes.

It shakes so much that Ana María calls from the house, "No touching the blacks!"

At least she can't see it was me.

"Probably waiting to interrupt my big scene,

142

like you did to Blair," Maddie grouses.

I want to tell her that I have better things to do, but that's not actually true. Still, I don't even know what her big scene is. Honestly, she's more self-involved than the male engineers who didn't even bother designing a space suit that would fit a female astronaut.

I don't want Maddie to think she's gotten the best of me, but it's better than standing here listening to her accusations, so I move to the back of the theater. The loading dock door is open, airing out the paint fumes.

It's almost never open, which is why I hadn't thought of this before, but it's perfect. I slip outside and breathe in the fresh, paint-free, Maddie-free air. Then I walk around the block to the front of the theater.

Where the lobby doors are locked.

It's okay, though. I'll sit on the bench next to the box office until someone shows up to open them. We've gotten far enough into summer that lots of tourists are walking up and down the street, oohing and aahing at how quaint the island is. I watch them go by and make guesses about where they come from, and how badly they've screwed up, and if they've ever tried to keep a loved one from leaving and succeeded.

Soon enough, Mrs. Freymiller appears with more garment bags.

"Zadie!" she says. "What are you doing out here?"

"Staying out of the way."

She frowns, pulling a key from the folds of her billowy cardigan. She unlocks the door, and I hold it open for her.

"I'm really sorry, Mrs. Freymiller." I never got to say that after I messed up the costumes. And the wigs. "I honestly wasn't trying to ruin your designs."

"Of course not, love." Inside the lobby, she readjusts the garment bags in her arms. "You know there are very few things in life that can't be fixed with the right spirit and determination. I've got both in spades. And you know what? So do you."

She winks and then sails through the curtains dividing the lobby from the theater.

If only that were true. I don't think spirit and determination are going to keep Grandma Sooz on Bainbridge Island.

15
Respect Each Other's Dressing Spaces

The next day after rehearsal, I climb into Jacob's minivan with Zach. It smells like feet and grass and juice boxes, thanks to Micah, Jasmine, and Namina, who have all been picked up from soccer camp right before us.

"Miss Zadie!" Jacob booms as I buckle in. "How is my favorite future shuttle commander?"

Before I can answer him:

"Zadie, I got two goals today!"

"Want a juice box, Zadie?"

"My team lost our scrimmage, Zadie."

I am immediately reminded why Zach needs

his own room. And this is before we get back to his house and I meet Arlo and Penny. Who are screaming their adorable little heads off while Jim carefully transfers a gelatinous blob from the kombucha he's brewing into a clean jar.

"Dinner in twenty minutes," Jim calls after us as Zach drags me to the stairs to show me the progress on his attic room.

It's totally different from the last time I saw it, a dark, dusty jumble of piled-up boxes. That stuff has all been cleared out to make room for Zach's furniture. They've laid down a bright blue carpet and put in a window at one end, so natural light floods in.

"They're going to put in a window at the other end too," Zach says. "Then it'll be pretty much done."

He has way more space than he did when he was crammed into a tiny room downstairs with Micah. There his only privacy was a bottom bunk with curtains he drew around it; he was basically in a pod the size of the astronaut's personal areas on the International Space Station.

Here, he could practice show choreography!

"This is so cool!" I flop onto his bed and try to imagine having my own room, instead of a room with half the walls covered in Broadway show posters and half covered in NASA posters, constantly getting nagged by Lulu to pick up my stuff or leave her alone.

But I would share with Lulu forever if it meant Grandma Sooz would stay in the basement. We're lucky to have a house at all. And if Mom loses her job . . .

Zach might have plenty of space in his new room, but at dinner everyone squeezes around a table that wasn't really made for an extra guest. Jim tries to coax the twins to put some of the spaghetti in their mouths instead of their hair, while the three middle kids chatter about soccer camp.

When there's finally a lull in the conversation, Jacob asks about some of Papa's music students who he knows from teaching at the high school. Which leads to me explaining how Papa's driving for Ryde now, which leads to concerned looks from both dads.

I see my chance.

"Which means it's a good thing Mom has her job at BYT," I say pointedly, keeping my eyes on my fork as I twirl my noodles. "And that it's a totally secure job that gives us health insurance and all."

There's a pause. I'm aware it's a weird thing to say. But I'm also aware that Jim's on the island council. The island council that's considering whether or not Mom gets to keep her job.

"What was that about at dinner?" Zach asks as they walk me home, Jacob way behind us, pushing the twins in a giant double-wide stroller.

I glance over my shoulder to see if there's any chance Jacob will hear me. Then I come clean about the threat to my mom's job from the island council.

"And you think my dad wouldn't stand up for your mom without you reminding him?"

Now that he puts it that way, it seems dumb. But Jim is a city planner, not an arts guy.

"I don't know how much he cares about the theater!"

"Enough that I do it all year round."

"Yeah, but . . ."

Zach waits. He's good at letting people talk instead of jumping in to fill the silence.

"But you're the only one in your whole family who does arts stuff."

Zach shoots me a weird look. "Just because they don't do it doesn't mean they don't appreciate it for me. Look, Zadie, it probably wouldn't be right for him to fight for your mom's job because we're friends. Or because they're friends. But he would fight for it because he believes in the theater. I know he does. The thing is, he's just one member of the council."

Zach's right. And the whole way to convince the entire council to keep funding Mom's job is to make sure *Spinderella* goes off without a flaw in the design.

16
Just Don't

The next day after snack, I end up in the stage manager's booth. We're so close to opening. All I want to do is hide out somewhere no one will see me and I can't possibly mess anything up. Plus there's a beat-up recliner in the corner, which is incredibly comfortable, if you avoid the one giant spring that pokes out of the seat. A nap seems like the perfect way to pass this hour.

Even though Ana María has been getting a touch less frosty with me, I'd never go up to the booth if she were there. But she won't start running the show from the booth until next week. For now she's still sitting in the house next to Mom.

Her laptop is up in the booth, open, but the

screen is dark. Next to it is an OSF travel mug. There's no lid on the mug, and I peek in to see that it's half-full of coffee. An open container of liquid right next to an open laptop is a major safety hazard if I've ever seen one.

I don't trust myself to move the travel mug without somehow causing the accident I'm trying to avoid. With my luck, a massive earthquake would strike at exactly the moment I picked up the mug, and coffee would spill all over the computer. Of course, even without me touching the mug, an earthquake could strike and spill coffee all over the computer.

Instead I reach out and gently close the laptop. That way, if the coffee should spill, the only things that might be damaged are the cool stickers. I've caught glimpses of them before, but now I can see each one much more clearly.

There's an OSF sticker, of course. NO HUMAN IS ILLEGAL. The NASA one, plus a rainbow roller skate, which I noticed earlier, but up close I realize it says ROSE CITY ROLLERS along the wheels. And there's a tough-looking lady showing her bicep, and the words above her say, SÍ SE PUEDE.

On second thought, these stickers are too cool

to risk them getting ruined. In slow motion, like I'm Kate Rubins on a space walk, upgrading the Space Station's solar array, I move the laptop to the other side of the light board, far from the hazardous coffee.

I peer down from the booth at Ana María in the house. She's texting — of course — but she's also flipping pages in the script and leaning over to tell Mom something. She's so cosmically awesome.

I settle into the recliner and try to block out all the embarrassing, annoying things that have happened in this theater over the last few weeks. There is no way, however, to block out the scream that wakes me an hour later. "Scream" might not be the word. It's more of an agonized moan, a horrified wail of despair. It's Ana María, huddled over her laptop.

"Did the coffee spill?" I ask, popping up. "Was there an earthquake?"

"An earthquake?!"

"Is everything okay?" Mom's voice calls from below the booth.

"No!" Ana María shouts. "No! Nothing is okay!"

I sink back into the chair, wishing I could

melt through the floor. I don't know what's gone wrong, and Ana María is blocking the only way out of the booth. Mom almost never comes up here, because you have to climb a ladder mounted on the wall, and her knees don't like that. But I hear her creaking her way up.

"Ana María?" Mom's head appears, and her eyes widen at the sight of me. "Oh no."

"I didn't do anything."

Ana María turns on me. "Didn't you?"

Mom hauls herself up into the booth. "Okay, let's take a beat—"

"You didn't touch anything?" Ana María demands, holding up her laptop.

"No! I swear! All I did was close it! To protect it! The mug—"

Ana María lets out a primal scream and then jams the laptop into her bag. "I'm out, Marinee," she says. Her face is bright red and tears spill over. Her hands are clenched tight, and she's the spitting image of Lulu when she realized I'd covered her favorite boots in duct tape. (I was making moon boots!) (I didn't know it would leave a gross, goopy, impossible-to-remove residue!)

"Ana María." Mom puts a calming hand on her arm, but Ana María jerks away. "It's going to be fine. Really. Whatever it is, Zadie and I will fix it—"

"Really? Does Zadie know how to rebuild a magic sheet? Do you?" she says.

"A magic sheet—"

"I'd just finished channeling when rehearsal started. I left it here to input into Excel later. No one else comes in the booth but me. But then your daughter came up here and messed with the computer and now look!"

She flings her hand toward the corner of the booth. The corner where it leaks when it rains. Like it's been doing for the last couple of days. Sure enough, there's a piece of notebook paper sitting in a puddle of water, all the ink muddled into a blob of blue.

"All I did was move the computer!"

"Yeah, well I'd set it under the computer for safekeeping. So you knocked it off the table when you moved the computer. That's hours down the drain."

"Ana María," my mom says. "I don't understand. I thought this was all computerized. Is one piece of paper really so—"

But Ana María's phone buzzes. Nobody else would dare check a text in the middle of an exchange like this with Mom, but I know Ana María will and Mom won't say anything.

She does, and then her bright red face goes totally white. "I have to go," she says.

And that's it. Ana María is gone. Probably for good. The show opens in a week. Tech is about to start, which is the busiest time, the time a show most desperately needs a stage manager, and Mom is on her own. It will absolutely be a disaster and the island council won't give the theater the funding it needs and Mom will lose her job.

Which means Grandma Sooz will definitely move to Florida.

And it is all my fault.

Nobody notices when I leave the theater. Or if they do, they're probably glad. I screw up everything I touch, even when I'm trying to be helpful. And I'm not only screwing up one show now. I'm screwing up whole lives. Ana María's. My family's. Grandma's.

I'm not sure where I'm going, only that I can't stay here.

I walk along Main Street, trying to avoid looking at the windows where Bainbridge shop owners let me tape up show posters. They just remind me of all the ways I've messed up. Of all the ways this show is going to be a disaster.

Each time I think about turning around and going back to the theater, my stomach flips. So I keep walking.

It's almost three miles to home, and besides, Papa's teaching piano lessons today. I can't face him. One look at me and he'll know I've done something horrible. Again.

But it's only about a mile to Zoom Zoom Zumba. When I get there, Grandma will text Mom to let her know where I am. I'm heading in the right direction, like my feet knew before my brain did that Grandma is the only person I can face right now. And soon she won't be there to turn to anymore.

The tears are close, I know it. I don't even bother fighting them.

A lady pushing a stroller approaches me as tears stream down my face. "Are you all right, honey?"

Obviously I am not all right. But I am not telling this random lady all the ways I have messed up. "Allergies," I say, and keep walking.

I saw this video once about how astronauts cry in space. The tears didn't fall, like mine are now. They just sort of globbed up into a blob of water attached to the astronaut's face. International Space Station Commander Chris Hadfield recorded it, and he had to use a dropper to put water in his eyes because he couldn't just cry real tears on command.

But I bet astronauts do cry in space. Just not when there are cameras recording. Because it's got to be lonely. Even if they are all crammed into a tight space with up to ten other people.

They go up there with a belief in the possibilities of what else exists. Because they've never quite felt like they fit on Earth. Like nobody else gets them, but maybe they'll fit among the stars. Then they get up there, and the stars are just hot balls of gas.

And there's still more space to explore, but they can't just throw on a space suit and check it out. There are protocols and limits and constant communication with the other astronauts and mission control back on Earth. So they're lonely, but they're also stuck with other people. That would make me cry for sure.

Grandma says, *The sky's the limit*, but the sky has limits too.

I can feel the stroller lady standing there, not moving on, but I keep walking. I scrub my face free of tears, so no one will stop me and insist on calling an adult.

Finally Zoom Zoom Zumba comes into view. All I want is to curl up in Grandma's office and cry until she comes in to hold me and then cry some more.

But when I reach the door, it's locked. And the studio is dark inside. Something is seriously wrong. It's not only that things are closed up. That happens. Occasionally Grandma has an appointment or something. But then I realize what's really wrong with this picture. To the right of the door, right next to the poster for Bainbridge Youth Theater's production of *Spinderella*, is another sign that shouts louder than anything else. It says, FOR SALE.

17
Get Enough Rest

When I see that FOR SALE sign, I lose it. I collapse in the studio doorway and sob. I sob hard enough that the florist next door comes out, and then some other people gather and murmur together about what to do with me, and then someone kneels next to me and I hear a familiar voice.

"Zadie?"

It's Zach's dad Jim. He's got the twins in their double stroller, and for once they're not screaming their heads off. They both look at me with wide eyes. One of them holds out a grubby stuffed bunny, like it might make me feel better.

"Honey, what's wrong?"

I'm still sobbing too hard to respond, but Jim tells the onlookers that he can get me home. Most of them know Jim—he is on the island council, after all—but the florist won't leave until Jim pulls up some photos on his phone of our families together. And then it's just me and Jim and Arlo and Penny. Jim sits on the sidewalk next to me.

"You've got a lot going on," he says.

I sniffle.

"Zach told us about your grandma's move."

The sobs threaten to return.

"It's so hard when people move away. The worst for me was after college. I'd finally found my people there, after being a total outcast in school. Never being close to my family. College was hard at first—I honestly didn't think I *could* make friends. But then I did. Incredible friends who really got me, you know? But we mostly went our separate ways when we graduated, and I thought I'd never find a group like that again."

"Let me guess," I said. "You did." Adults always have these stories with simple morals, like it's so easy for them to look back on how everything worked out exactly like it was supposed to.

"Not exactly," he says. "Not like that group. College is a really specific time. Living in dorms, studying together, figuring out what you want to do with your life. But I found Jacob. And we found Bainbridge. And we've built our community here. It's different, but it's good. Really good."

"I'm not going to find a different but good grandma."

"No," he says. "You're not."

"And I wouldn't want to."

"Of course you wouldn't," he says. "But you will find a new normal. And Jacob and I are here for you, any time you want to talk."

"Thanks, Jim."

We get up and start walking together toward the minivan, parked a few blocks away. I push the stroller while Jim texts my parents to let them know what's up. By the time we get the twins buckled into their car seats and make the short drive to my house, I've calmed down.

I think about bringing up the island council and the theater funding, but what is even the point? With the magic sheet debacle—whatever that is, I don't even understand, but it was enough to make Ana María quit — I've already ruined the show past anything Jim can do about it.

Papa's far from calm when he opens the door. I'm not sure I've ever been in this much trouble, including the time when I was seven and I got Zach to help me build a rocket ship out of his grandpa's riding lawn mower and then we crashed it into Jacob's new minivan.

Mom's more like furious when she gets home — how could I leave the theater without telling anyone and walk a mile and what was I thinking. It's so bad that Lulu leaves me alone in our room to think about what I've done, but I can still hear her in the backyard practicing her solo.

Her solo in the play I've ruined.

When Papa calls me for dinner, I tell him I'm not hungry. How can I eat when Grandma's about to move across the country? When the studio is for sale? When everything I know is changing faster than I can keep up? For all I know, grilled cheese sandwiches will suddenly taste disgusting.

Papa sits down on the edge of my bed and runs his hands over his face.

Finally, he says, "We didn't know she was putting the studio up for sale."

For a second I feel the tiniest bit better. But then: "But you knew she was moving out. Moving across the country! Why didn't you say something? Lulu and I deserve to know."

He sighs. "Nothing's a done deal. But I understand why you're upset. I was your age when my parents decided to move our family to the United States. They didn't warn us. I just got up one day and they handed me a packed backpack and we were off."

What I'm going through is nothing like having to suddenly leave everything I've ever known and make a dangerous journey to a place where I don't speak the language. I know that. But if Papa's point is to count your blessings, I tell you what: I am not in the mood.

Sometimes your problems aren't the biggest problems in the world, but they're still *your* biggest problem.

"I think they were trying to spare me the worry. Because I really didn't have a say in the decision, and there were reasons for leaving that I couldn't understand."

"But Grandma's not running away from war and poverty! She's running away from us!"

Then I'm crying again, and Papa doesn't try to teach me any more lessons. He sits with me and strokes my hair and softly sings this Guatemalan lullaby that tells kids to go to sleep before the wolves come and eat them, which is super messed up, but no more messed up than a princess being forced to marry by a certain age and then going into an enchanted sleep that can only be broken by the kiss of some dude she's never met and might not even want to kiss her.

I guess we all have our messed-up stories.

When Lulu finally comes to our room, she brings me a PB & J.

"Thanks." I eye the sandwich. The crusts are cut off, which Mom and Papa refuse to do, but Lulu also hates crusts. The rare thing we have in common. "Did you make this for me?"

She shrugs. "I figured you had to be hungry. Did you even have lunch?"

I shake my head and bite into the sandwich. It's the perfect ratio of PB to J, but not even that can lift my spirits.

Lulu flomps onto her bed. I think she's

despairing over how I've ruined the show, the one where she's finally getting to play a leading role, but then she says, "I can't believe Zoom Zoom Zumba is for sale."

Maybe she doesn't know about the magic sheet, or Ana María walking out. I'm not going to be the one to tell her. And anyway, Grandma's the bigger problem.

"And no one told us."

"Exactly."

She's still for a minute, and I try to chew as quietly as possible because I know mouth sounds super annoy Lulu, and she's actually being nice to me, so.

"And like"—she sits back up—"it has to mean she's moving, right? Why else would she put it up for sale?"

I don't say anything. Because there's nothing to say. There are no other reasons.

In the morning I don't get up when Lulu's alarm goes off. I don't get up when she comes back from the shower and throws her wet towel on top of me. And when Mom comes in to nag me out of bed, I don't even bother faking sick. I'm too bad an actor, and it's obvious why I can't show my face at the theater today.

"I'm not going," I say.

Mom sighs. "Papa has to drive today, and Grandma will be at the studio."

I guess Grandma hasn't shut the studio down completely. Yet. "I'm old enough to stay home alone."

Mom looks skeptical. She's left me home with Lulu, but not by myself. Not for a whole day. But she doesn't say no right away, so I know she's considering it. Probably better to risk me burning down the house than the theater.

"I swear I won't step foot outside or open the door, even. I won't use the stove. You can lock me in the bedroom, if you want."

"How would you pee?" Lulu asks as she gathers her things in her magic sequin backpack.

In outer space, astronauts collect their pee and recycle it into drinking water. I glance at the bottle on my bedside table, and Lulu makes a face.

Papa arrives for what's turned into a family meeting. "I could come home at lunchtime to check on her."

Mom pulls out her phone and fires off a text. "My mom could probably check on her once or twice." She looks at me. "And I will check in with you on the hour. You will answer my calls every time." She doesn't bother saying what the consequence will be if I don't, because we both know it would be like trying to reenter Earth's atmosphere without a heat shield.

Papa comes in and kisses me on the forehead. "Hang in there, Commander Zadie."

Lulu swings her backpack onto her shoulder and gives me a pitying look before heading out.

"And one more thing, Z," Mom says from the doorway. "This is only for today. Sometimes it's okay to wallow. But you have to face the music eventually."

If you had asked me a week ago what I would do if I had the whole house to myself for an entire day, my plans would have included using all Lulu's makeup to do gory alien special effects on my face, playing with Papa's super-intricate collectible Lego sets, locating all of Mom's secret chocolate stashes, and making the ooey-gooiest ice cream sundae/sugar cereal/chocolate explosion you've ever seen.

But now? I don't do any of that. I do exactly what Mom said: I wallow.

The day is long and boring, but so are my days at the theater. At least at home I'm not going to mess anything up, and the only person I have to serve snack to is myself. Papa pops in at lunchtime like he promised, but he only stays for a minute to make sure I'm okay, and then he has to pick up another passenger.

Grandma Sooz drops in around three, and I am not proud of this, but I pretend I'm asleep. She comes into the room, and the mattress dips as she sits on the edge of my bed.

"Oh, Zig-Zag," she says quietly. "This is all so hard. I'm trying to do what's right, to help this family. But it's hurting you. You'll never know how sorry I am for that."

She smooths my hair off my face, while I fight to keep completely still. Finally she kisses my forehead and leaves the room. When I go out to the kitchen later, there's a snickerdoodle from my favorite bakery, with a note that says, *You're an incredible kid and that's a fact. G.S.*

At dinnertime I'm still in my pajamas, but I come out to eat, since it turns out all-day cereal and giant snickerdoodles are not the most satisfying diet. Mom frowns at my pajamas but doesn't say anything, and everyone talks about their day like it was totally normal.

Apparently it was. Rehearsal was smooth, no disasters. I mean, obviously, since I wasn't there. The cast has the next two days off while Mom and the designers do tech stuff at the theater, and then on Monday tech week begins.

I'm too chicken to ask how they're managing without Ana María. Instead, I shovel my dinner down, excuse myself, and go back to bed.

18
Acting Is Reacting

On Saturday Lulu and I stay home with Papa while Mom spends the day at the theater. She and Fiona will get the set loaded in so that when the actors get there on Monday, they'll finally be able to rehearse on the real set. It seems to me like all acting is pretending anyway, but Lulu says it makes a big difference to act a scene with the actual furniture, instead of random chairs bunched together to form a rehearsal bed or whatever.

With the set in place, Mom and the designers will build the cues, which means going through every lighting and sound cue and checking that they look right and sound right and making whatever adjustments are required. There's no need for all the actors to stand around while they do that, although there have been times in the past when Lulu and I hung around to be bodies on the stage, so the designers didn't have to imagine how it would work with actors.

(The absolute-no-doubt-about-it best was when I got to stand in for the Wicked Witch of the West during the *I'm melting* scene, and over and over I got to melt down into the trapdoor and then come back up and do it again.)

No big shocker that Mom didn't ask me to come today.

Lulu's exhausted from rehearsals and was still in bed when Mom left. I'm wide-awake, though. After a day of doing absolutely nothing, I'm buzzing with energy.

I try putting Sir Andrew Lloyd Webber in the cat harness Mom refused to buy on the principle that he would never in a million years tolerate it so I saved up my own money and bought it myself, and just like every other time I've tried it, he sits immobile and levels me with a death glare that could take out an entire alien race.

I do some chores, figuring maybe I'll get back

in Mom's good graces (at least a little bit), and it's pretty hard to screw up unloading the dishwasher. Then I drop Mom's KAMALA HARRIS FOR THE PEOPLE mug. Only a cosmic miracle keeps it from breaking, but it's enough to put me off doing chores.

Finally evening comes. Papa gets home, and we're rolling out the dough for his amazing homemade pizza when the garage door creaks open. He glances at the clock. "A little earlier than expected. That must mean things went well today."

I nod, whacking at the dough with the rolling pin. "No one around to distract them."

He sighs and kisses my head, then turns on the oven to preheat.

"It smells delicious," Mom says as she walks in.

"Oh wow, it sure does."

I freeze at the second voice. My back is to the door, a ladleful of pizza sauce in my hand.

"Hi there, welcome. I'm Felipe. You must be Ana María!"

I concentrate on spreading the sauce evenly across the dough as I try to figure out what is going on. Ana María is here?

"It's nice to meet you," she says, and she doesn't

even sound mad. "It's so nice of you to invite me for dinner."

"You're welcome any time!"

"Zadie?" Mom steps up next to me and bumps my hip with hers. "Can you say hello?"

I turn slowly to peek at Ana María. She holds up a hand in a tiny wave, looking a little shy too. "Hey," she says.

"Hey."

We face off for another second before she turns back to Papa. "Anything I can do to help?"

He waves her away, insisting she and Mom sit. He pours them each a glass of wine and makes a big deal over serving them.

I spread the cheese next, and then the sausage, and then another layer of cheese. As soon as the pizza is ready to go in the oven, I flee from the kitchen.

"Ana María is here," I announce as I burst into our room and shut the door behind me.

Lulu's sitting cross-legged on her bed, writing out note cards to each cast member for opening night. She's been working on them all day. She only looks mildly surprised. "Really?"

"For dinner, I guess? She's acting like nothing's wrong!"

Lulu looks up at me, confused. "What would be wrong?"

"Well, I mean, she quit! Because of me! Now there's no stage manager and Mom's left totally hanging and—"

Lulu drops her pen. "What are you talking about? Ana María quit? When?"

"After I screwed everything up?"

"Which time?"

I grab my stuffed space shuttle and throw it at her. "With the magic sheet! On Thursday!"

Lulu throws the shuttle back at me. "I don't know what a magic sheet is, but Ana María was there as usual for Friday's rehearsal. Remember, when you faked sick?"

"I didn't fake sick!"

"Whatever. And she was there today, too. I called Mom at lunchtime and heard Ana María in the background." She gathers her note cards into a neat stack and sets them on her perfectly organized desk. "Whatever you think happened wasn't as terrible as your overactive imagination has made it out to be, Z."

And then she leaves me alone to wonder how in the galaxy I could have gotten everything so incredibly wrong.

At dinner, Ana María sits in Grandma Sooz's spot, directly across from me. No one says where Grandma is tonight, or explains why Ana María is there for dinner.

They don't talk about the show, either—Mom laid that ground rule down right after we said grace. "No talking shop tonight!" she said, raising her wine glass.

Once Papa discovered that Ana María speaks Spanish, he was off, talking in the animated way he reserves for conversations with other native speakers. His volume goes up; his hands get more active. Mom can speak fluently, from a year in Guatemala after college, but it's different with a native speaker.

Normally I might feel a little left out, since I mostly understand but don't speak super well. But tonight, it's fine by me to sit there and listen.

Ana María's accent is different from Papa's Guatemalan one, but I can still understand her. She and her parents moved here from Oaxaca, Mexico, when she was a toddler, she tells Papa.

Lots of her family are still there, but they brought her grandfather up as soon as they'd saved enough money to sponsor his immigration.

When Ana María was away at college, her parents got divorced and her dad moved back to Mexico. But then her mom got sick with cancer. Ana María almost quit school to come home and take care of her, but her mom insisted she finish her education. Then she insisted Ana María take the opportunity to work at the Oregon Shakespeare Festival when it came up. This was why they had sacrificed everything to come to the United States—so Ana María could have the best education and follow her dreams.

A life in the theater wasn't exactly the stable, prosperous American dream Ana María's mother had envisioned, but she also saw how good her daughter was at her job and made her promise never to stop following her dream. Which is why Ana María stayed at OSF even when her mom passed away.

But that left her grandfather here alone, and when his health started to decline, Ana María had no choice but to come home and care for him.

Like Papa, she's more animated when she speaks in Spanish. There's none of the hyper-controlled stage manager in how she talks, or reaches for another slice of pizza, or jokes with Lulu. Even though her story is sad, she's relaxed. She's comfortable here, with us.

"Who's with your grandfather tonight?" I ask.

Everyone looks at me in surprise. I guess it's the first thing I've said, and maybe it sounded rude, like I was judging her for leaving him alone. But I didn't mean it like that. I'm thinking about Grandma Sooz, not too far in the future, when she'll be alone at a retirement home in Florida.

"Zadie!" Mom says.

"No, Marinee, it's okay. It's a good question. My aunt actually flew out from Arizona to help during tech week, since we knew I'd be extra busy. She's an ER nurse and can't usually get away, but she's using some vacation time."

"Oh," I say. "That's nice of her."

"Yeah," Ana María says with a sad sort of smile. "It's really nice having some family around."

Lulu catches my eye, and we're both thinking the same thing. Soon we'll have even less family around. As it is, lots of Papa's family is in a whole other country. But we've always had Grandma Sooz.

And we've got Mom and Papa. Ana María doesn't have anyone.

"I'm sorry he's sick," I say.

Before Ana María can respond, Mom lets out a gigantic yawn, slapping her hand over her mouth in embarrassment.

"Oh my gosh, I'm so sorry," she says. "It's been a long day."

"It sure has." Ana María pushes back from her chair. "I think that's my cue."

"Exit stage left," Papa says with a chuckle.

"Don't let me chase you off," Mom says. "You should stay, keep chatting with Felipe. But I think I need to excuse myself."

"No, really." Ana María stands. "I'm exhausted too. It was so nice of you all to include me for dinner. But I'm going to call myself a ride."

"No, no," Papa says. "I'll give you a ride home."

"That's really okay." Ana María pulls out her phone and opens the rideshare app. "You've been driving people around all day. Plus I really like rideshares. You meet the most interesting people." She glances at the screen, and then at me. "Zadie, it'll be a few minutes before the car gets here. Would you wait with me out on the porch?"

I look at Mom with a question in my eyes. She gives a quick nod and then stands to hug Ana María.

"We're almost there. I'm so glad to have you on board."

"Thanks, Marinee. Good night, everyone."

Ana María walks to the door and holds it open for me. "What do you say, Zadie?"

Out on the porch, the sky is just starting to get dark in that strange Pacific Northwest summer sort of way where it feels like six until way after bedtime.

"It's so beautiful up here," Ana María says, settling onto our porch swing. "You're lucky."

"Isn't it like Ashland?" I ask. Oregon isn't that far away. I always imagined it was sort of like Washington South.

"It's similar. But there's something about being on the island. Seattle's just a ferry ride away, but I like how Bainbridge feels set apart from the rest of the world."

"Yeah. Me too." We sit in silence for a minute. I hope it's not an awkward silence. For me it feels kind of nice. "I'm sorry if it was rude to ask about your grandpa."

"It wasn't."

"You don't have to say that. I know I'm always screwing everything up."

"What? No, you're not."

I give her the kind of look Lulu gives me when I swear I won't ever ask her for anything ever again if she'll let me have the last ice cream bar in the package.

She laughs. "Okay, okay. You have . . . presented some challenges. But you've always been trying to help."

"Just because I mean well doesn't mean I haven't been driving you crazy."

"You really haven't. Life has been challenging me in a million more ways than you or anything at BYT. Sometimes it all kind of hits at once, you know?"

Do I ever.

"Honestly, Zadie, you're a bright spot."

"I am?"

"You are. You remind me of me."

She pauses, and I'm afraid to ask what she means by that. There's no way super-competent Ana María, who's always on top of everything and dropped her whole life to selflessly take care of her grandpa, is anything like me.

"I used to do roller derby. Did you know that?"

That's not what I expected her to say. And I don't know what that has to do with me.

"I'm not coordinated," I say. "I could never do roller derby."

She gives a little shrug. "You might be surprised. I started doing it in high school. There was a lot of family stuff going on, and I was pretty angry. Most of the time. And I thought, hey, there's an activity where the whole point is slamming into people? Sign me up."

"Let me guess: There's more to it than that?"

She grins. "There is and there isn't. I mean, yeah, there's teamwork and leadership skills and getting seriously strong inside and out. But also? It's about slamming into people. At least if you're a blocker, which I was."

I think back to reading *Roller Girl* and the

Derby Daredevils. "Those are the ones who keep the opposing team away from the girl trying to get through, right?"

"Yep, the jammer. As blockers, our whole job is knocking the other blockers out of the way, or knocking out the other jammer. So it is about slamming into people. But there's a point to it. It's not only barreling into people for no reason, or to hurt someone. We're trying to accomplish something."

It sounds cosmically awesome, though I'm 100 percent sure I would break all my bones if I tried to get on roller skates. "What does this have to do with me?"

"Well, it's true that you've sort of . . . barreled into stuff around the theater this summer."

I wince.

"But it hasn't been pointless," she hurries to say. "You definitely haven't been trying to hurt anyone. I think mostly you've hurt yourself. Which is also sort of like roller derby, before you learn to fall small. And even sometimes after. But you've really been trying to accomplish something, haven't you? That matters."

I have. At first I was just trying to figure out how to survive the summer in an atmosphere as inhospitable as Venus. (To me, anyway.) Then I wanted to prove I wasn't as much of a disaster as my mom thought I was, that I wasn't out to sabotage anything or anyone. And now so much more is on the line—my mom's job and the theater itself! And while it's clear that the best way I can help is to stay out of it, Ana María's the brightest hope for the show to be a success.

"Did you always do tech?" I ask, wondering how long it will take her ride to arrive. I hope they get a flat tire.

"I started when I was around your age."

"But I mean, did you never want to perform?"

"Oh! No, never. Anyone can perform. Literally. Ever heard of dancing monkeys?"

I bark out a laugh and she grins.

"I'm joking. No disrespect to actors. They do their own kind of hard work. But techies? We know how to make magic so intricate that people don't realize they're seeing it. A really complicated show, a big musical with lots of sound cues and light cues and set changes? No one ever says, 'Wow, the stage manager did a heck of a job calling that show.' They don't ever realize how much the show relies on what I do."

It's kind of like all the folks who work at NASA but aren't astronauts. People who plan missions and build rockets and design space suits. The people at mission control who can see the big picture, and who can fix problems from thousands of miles away are basically stage managers.

But the astronauts get all the glory.

"Doesn't that bug you, though? Not getting credit?"

"I don't do it for credit. I do it because I love the magic. I love seeing how the magic affects the audience. I love supporting actors and designers in what they do. That's enough for me."

I think about that. I don't want to act on a stage. But I do like presenting at Science Kidz or belt ceremonies at tae kwon do. I like being recognized for the stuff I'm good at. Maybe that's part of why this summer has been so hard. Not only have I not been able to do the stuff I'm good at, but I've been bad at the stuff I've been stuck doing.

"Still, I'm really sorry if I've made anything harder for you. Especially the magic sheet."

"I'm sorry too. I came here in a bad headspace, and honestly things haven't gotten any easier. But it's not because of you. I think maybe, instead of trying to do everything myself, I should take advantage of a capable, enthusiastic assistant stage manager who's sitting around the theater, waiting to help."

"Assistant stage manager?"

"What do you think? I thought you could start by coming in tomorrow and helping me rebuild the magic sheet."

"Are you serious? What about my mom? She's got this thing about kids—"

"—in tech. I know. Kind of like my thing about no kids in the booth. We all make mistakes. Or maybe it's that some rules are meant to be bent."

Not in space. In space you have to follow the protocols or you could die. Of course, Valentina Tereshkova's ship was programmed to steer her out of Earth's orbit and never go back down. If she'd followed the plan, she would have died.

"Plus women in theater tech need to stick together."

"Yeah?" At the beginning of the summer, I

wouldn't have even called myself a woman—or girl—in theater tech.

"Yeah! And Latinas in tech even more. BYT is really unusual with your mom at the helm, hiring me. Women designers in every discipline. Did you know ninety percent of master electricians are male?"

"Really?"

"Yup. When you look at theater designers, around seventy percent of them are male. It's even higher for lighting and sound."

"Not costume, though."

Ana María turns her gaze from the hazy evening sky to look at me directly. "No, not costumes. Costume designers are seventy percent female."

"So that's good."

"It's . . . complicated. Sure, it's great for the women who want to be costume designers. But why do you think costume designers are mostly women and lights and sound are mostly men?"

I shift uncomfortably, thinking about how I scorned costume design as the least interesting part of theater tech.

Ana María's phone buzzes as a squatty blue

car pulls up at the curb. "That's my ride," she says. "Think about that, and we'll talk more tomorrow. If you'll take the job as my ASM?"

I grin. "I'm in."

She stands and heads for the car but turns back. "Want to know a secret?"

I shoot to my feet, trying to squash my impulse to rocket across the lawn. "Yes."

"The lighting grid is my favorite place in the world too."

19

Fix Your Mistakes

I know the minute I step inside that hanging out at Bainbridge Youth Theater with nobody but Ana María is going to be the coolest thing I've ever done (and I've won a battle of the bands with Zach, Jacob, and Grandma Sooz as my bandmates).

Mom dropped me off, but then she went back home to have her only day off in forever. Meanwhile, Ana María and I went inside the almost pitch-dark theater. Almost, because the theater is never completely dark. That's why there's a ghost light.

"It's just us, ghosties!" I call as we walk into

the theater, lit only by the bare bulb glowing on a stand in the middle of the stage.

"You know the ghost light is purely practical, right?" Ana María says, flipping on the boring house lights. "It's for safety reasons, so someone who wanders in when it's dark doesn't trip over a cord or fall into the orchestra pit."

"We don't have an orchestra pit," I say, climbing the stairs to the stage. "And for someone interested in space travel, you have a terrible imagination."

She laughs and sets her things down on the table set up in the middle of the audience as a makeshift desk for Mom and Ana María during tech.

I cross the stage to the ghost light. "The ghost light," I say as I drag it over to the wings, a job Mom has let me do since I was big enough, "is necessary to keep the ghosts company when no one else is in the theater."

"You don't think they can see in the dark?"

"These are ghosts of actors, Ana María," I holler as I unplug the light and leave it in the corner of the wings. "They lived in the spotlight.

They could survive in the dark, but they'd get lonely. Restless. Who knows what would happen then? You think I can wreak havoc. Imagine a theater full of neglected actor ghosts!"

"Oof," Ana María says. "You've convinced me."

We spend the next three hours working on stage manager stuff. Ana María starts with teaching me what a magic sheet is: a single piece of paper with the grid location of each lighting instrument, what that lighting instrument does, and which dimmer it's attached to, so it can be controlled from the stage manager's booth. Like everything else now, that info gets put into a computer spreadsheet. But Ana María learned from an old-school master electrician, so she always notes it down by hand and transfers it later.

"Better that than drop an iPad from the grid," she points out.

The puddle incident happened in between writing everything down—which takes hours— and entering it into the computer. Which is why Ana María was so upset when she discovered the ruined magic sheet. But it turns out to be awesome for me, because she walks me through how it's done and actually lets me help.

"Bring up channel one," she tells me, clicking something on the computer. Then she points to the light board with a billion different levers. The first dimmer is on the top left. I'm trying to be cool, but I 100 percent feel like an astronaut setting off on a voyage. "Next stop: the universe," I whisper as I push the lever for channel one up to the top.

Ana María grins. "No fear, no limits."

I might explode from happiness.

"Okay, look. Let's see what lights channel one turned on." We both peer through the window at the lights shining on the stage.

"Upstage left," I say.

"Good, those are called ellipsoidals. So we mark where they are on the magic sheet and note that they're channel one."

It takes us a couple of hours to rebuild the whole thing. My heart is in orbit, and even Ana María seems like she's having fun. At least it doesn't seem like she regrets inviting me. Probably it's taking longer than it would if she just did it herself. But I am hanging on her every word; even if she doesn't care about credit, sometimes it can feel nice to know you're appreciated.

We have just enough time before Papa picks me up to head down to the dressing room and get the racks of clothes organized with labels with each cast member's name to the left of where their costumes hang. I've been in the dressing rooms a million times, and never once have I thought about who has to hang those labels.

"Did you think about what I said about costume designers?" Ana María says as she hands me Blair's name label. "Why they're mostly women?"

"Yeah." I actually thought about it a ton, but I still haven't quite figured out how to put it into words. "I think it has something to do with clothes being, like . . . girly. Whatever that means."

"Exactly. Whatever that means. A lot of people consider making clothes to be 'women's work.'" She shudders at the phrase. "And the same people see things like lights and sound—even more now that they're super computerized—to be 'men's work.' Which is why those disciplines are valued more. Considered 'real tech.' But like I told you on costume-parade day, costume design is just as demanding as any other kind of tech."

I think about it as we finish with the labels and trudge back upstairs.

"Is it changing, though?" I ask. "At NASA, it used to be that only men could be astronauts. Then, when they let women in, it was only a small number of them, compared to the men. But the most recent group to graduate is seven men and five women! Almost half!"

"That's awesome," she says. "I hope it's changing in theater tech. The best way I know how to help it change is to support other young women who I think would make awesome techies. Especially young women of color. I know you have different dreams, but as long as you're hanging around this planet, I'd love to keep showing you the ropes."

Lulu is a mess of nerves on Monday morning. She won't stop bouncing her knee and shaking the table as she eats her cereal.

"Do you mind?" I ask as the milk in my own bowl sloshes from side to side.

She shoots me a glare and turns up the volume on whatever she's listening to. Probably her own voice, singing in her ears. I don't think she's listened to anything else all summer.

I reach out and tug one of the earbuds out. "I think you know the words by now."

She shoves it back in. "You don't know anything, Zadie."

"Rude."

She frowns and starts bouncing her knee again. I reach for her earbud cord, and she slaps my hand away.

"Ow!"

"Don't touch my stuff!"

"Don't shake the table!"

"Girls, girls, girls!" Grandma Sooz walks into the kitchen, her hair a vibrant shade of pink. "What is going on in here?"

"Grandma, your hair!"

Grandma's new do is enough for Lulu to finally pull out her earbuds.

Grandma pats her hair a little self-consciously. "What do you think? I thought I'd try something new."

New like moving all the way across the country? I guess it makes sense to spruce herself up if she's getting ready to strike out and meet all new people and make new friends. Maybe all the old people in Florida have candy-colored hair, and she wants to fit in.

"I like it," Lulu says, but even she's not a good enough actor to hide the fact that she's thinking the same things I am. She stomps to the sink and drops her still mostly full cereal bowl in with a clatter.

"Is she getting the tech week nerves?" Grandma asks when Lulu's left the room.

"Why would she be nervous about tech? It's not like it's opening night or something. It's mostly standing around."

"Haven't you ever noticed?" Grandma says, futzing with the coffeepot. "Lulu always gets most nervous at the beginning of tech week. During *The Sound of Music* she threw up every morning. Once the show opened, she was fine."

How in the galaxy have I never noticed that, when I share a tiny room with her? When Grandma's gone, who will notice these things?

"Does Mom get nervous about tech too?"

"Your mom?" Grandma waves a hand. "Nah, she's fine during tech. But ooo-wheee, you know what she's like on opening night."

I really don't.

Grandma sees my face and goes on. "I think she gets more nervous than all the actors combined. After all, once the show starts, she no longer has any control over anything. It's out of her hands. Which is why she bites her cuticles down to bloody nubbins by the end of the first act."

Grandma sits, and I reach out to grab her hand. Her nails match her hair.

"Grandma," I say, commanding my voice not to wobble. "I don't want you to go anywhere."

"Oh Zig-Zag. I don't want to either."

I'm checking the presets for the final dress rehearsal—which means making sure that everything is where it's supposed to be at the top of the show, like the scepter that needs to be propped up next to King Horace's throne at the beginning, but has been moved offstage by the end of every run through—when Zach comes running up to me, wearing his King Horace breeches and a *Hadestown* T-shirt.

I narrow my eyes. "You should be fully in costume."

"No time," he pants, grabbing my hand and yanking me off the stage.

"What in the galaxy—"

"It's Mair and Baddie!"

I trip after him. "Blair and Maddie?"

"Right, whatever." He comes to a stop outside the girls' dressing room. "They've planned something awful."

It only takes him a minute to explain, and another minute for us to figure out what to do next.

"Five minutes to places," Ana María's voice says over the PA system.

If I take the time to go get her or Mom, they might not believe me and would just start the run. And even if they did, Lulu would get caught in the crossfire and might never recover. I'm the only one who can go in the girls' dressing room, so it's up to me to handle this. And I absolutely cannot mess it up.

I go straight to Lulu. "I'm not sure I got your presets right. Can you go check your props?"

She looks skeptical, since I haven't messed up any presets all week, but she's not going to risk it. As soon as she's gone, I corner Blair and Maddie.

"Hand them over," I say quietly. The other girls watch curiously, but I'd rather avoid making this a huge thing that could get back to Lulu. Even the thought of it would throw her off for the rest of the run.

"What are you even talking about?" They exchange looks that are guiltier than when the Russians blamed Valentina Tereshkova for the massive programming error that could have killed her.

"You know exactly what I'm talking about. Hand them over now and I won't go straight to my mom."

Blair holds my gaze, but Maddie cracks. She reaches into the folds of her Queen Lavinia dress and pulls out a tiny plastic container. Full of spiders.

Which I take straight to Ana María, because I only promised not to go to my mom. There's no way I'm going to let my bug-phobic sister pour a bottle full of live spiders out onstage when she's supposed to be making Spinderella's sleeping potion.

"They were smart," I tell Ana María as we march from the booth to backstage. "They were waiting until the show started to put them in the potion bottle, because otherwise I'd notice at pre-checks. And they were even smarter to do the whole prank during final dress."

"Why?"

"If they saved it for opening, it would entirely ruin the show. Probably stop it. Lulu would have a full-on panic attack, and they know it. If they get that over with today, by tomorrow, Lulu's the only one who'll still be freaking out, so her performance will suck and they can shine."

We've reached the dressing room. Ana María shakes her head. "Incredibly devious. And incredibly smart of you."

"Lulu can't know," I remind her as she opens the door.

"Hey, everybody, slight delay," she says, sticking her head in casually. "Ten more minutes. Blair and Maddie, can I see you for a second? Marinee wants me to go over the dance sequence with you one last time."

Have I mentioned how much I love Ana María?

As they follow her out of the dressing room, they're too terrified to even bother glaring at me. From down the hall at the boys' dressing room, Zach throws his arms wide like his siblings' favorite soccer player, Megan Rapinoe, when she gets a goal. I grin and shoot him a thumbs-up.

Ana María delivers Bladdie straight to my mom. I know better than to join the conversation, but I can hear them from the wings. Good thing Lulu's back in the dressing room.

The lecture about professionalism, maturity, and complete betrayal of the teamwork spirit of theater is a glorious thing to behold. And that's just Mom. After she marches off, too overcome to stand the sight of them a moment longer, Ana María starts in.

Mom's speech was good, but Ana María understands how girls like Blair and Maddie work.

"This kind of nasty behavior has no place in the theater. Or anywhere. But especially the theater.

Actors are asked to be open and vulnerable on that stage. They can't do that if they can't trust that everyone around them has their backs. And if you don't have their backs, they aren't going to have yours, and you'll never have a chance at being good. That's what you want, isn't it? To be the stars?"

They stare at her until they realize she's not going to continue until they respond. They both nod meekly.

"That's what I thought. Lulu Gonzalez gets that. Not only is she extremely talented, but she's in it to make sure everybody on that stage shines. You'll never get there if you keep this up. So no more pranks. No more targeting Lulu—or anyone else—and absolutely no blowback on Zadie for this either. I'll know. Even if she doesn't tell me. And I'll make sure Marinee never casts you at BYT again. Do you understand me?"

I get it now. Lulu's never going to know this happened. She's never going to know my part in saving her from it so she could go on and shine like she deserves. And that's okay. Because her awesome performance will be enough for me.

(It doesn't hurt that Blair and Maddie look like they could melt through the trapdoor right now.)

Opening night comes, and I see that Grandma Sooz was exactly right. Lulu wakes up beaming, and as soon as I'm up she makes my bed for me. At breakfast, she lets me have the last toaster pastry, and she even listens to *In the Heights* instead of her own voice.

Meanwhile, Mom has huge bags under her eyes, and the unnerving green tint to her skin is the exact shade of Queen Brunhilda's gown. Lulu offers to make her a cup of tea.

We get to the theater early, but it's already buzzing. Though that might be because of a glitch in the sound system that Ana María is frantically trying to fix.

"Hey there." Mom puts a calming hand on her shoulder. She's freaked too, but it helps her to have something productive to do. "How are you? Can I help you with that?"

Ana María looks up. Her eyes are red. Whether she was crying over this sound issue or something else, there's no doubt she's been crying. There's no hint of the fierce roller derby blocker knocking out Bladdie yesterday.

"Let me rephrase that," Mom says. "I'm going to take over with this." She gently nudges Ana María to the side. "Girls," she says to me and Lulu, "can you do a sweep of the house and make sure there aren't any stray things left out in the audience? Water bottles, jackets, whatever?"

I half expect Lulu to object; she's not only an actor, she's a lead actor. Picking up water bottles is so not her job. But she jumps into action. Probably being here an hour earlier than everyone else gives her more time to get nervous. My mom isn't the only one who likes to have a task.

Cleaning up the house only takes us a few minutes. I find a disturbing number of candy wrappers, considering I haven't given candy to anyone except Zach for weeks. When we're done, I go backstage with Lulu and do some straightening in the dressing room. Again with the candy wrappers! But when cast members start trickling in, I get out of there. Nervous actors are not my cup of tea.

I pass Zach on my way up the stairs. "Hey, Zach," I say. "How're you feeling?"

He grins, but it's not his usual grin. "You know, like I might puke at any moment," he says cheerfully.

I put a few more stairs between us. "Okay then, break a leg!"

Why anyone would choose to do a thing that makes them feel like they're going to hurl is beyond me. Not even choose to do it, but compete to do it! Then again, blasting off in a rocket ship might make me a little queasy, but I'd do whatever it took to get there.

Back in the theater, Mom has fixed the sound system glitch, so the only sound is the actors on the stage warming up. Blair and Maddie are both doing yoga-looking moves and making loud whoops and trills with their voices.

I pierce them with death glares from the wings until they feel my power and turn. I raise my eyebrows, my gaze stony. They both shrink back a little. I'm going to be watching them, and they know it. Exactly how I like it.

Satisfied, I grab a broom from where it's

propped in the corner and sweep the stage, giving the actors plenty of space to do their (superweird) thing.

"Zadie," Mom calls as I finish up. "Would you make sure Daniel practices his juggling sequence one more time?"

"Sure thing!"

I've never felt more useful! And while Mom is still a strange shade of green, she's looking better than she did at home. Here there are still things she has control of, at least until the show starts, and then it's all up to the actors. And stage management!

Once I've tracked Daniel down and watched his juggling sequence three times, I head up to the booth. Ana María's there, but she's not running through her preshow checks like I expected. Instead, she's buried in her phone.

"Are you okay?"

Her gaze snaps up. "I'm fine! Why does everyone keep asking that?"

"Because you look like you've been crying?"

She scowls. "Allergies."

I highly doubt that's the actual truth. I sit

quietly for a minute, not wanting to bug her. But I've been so helpful up until now. Adrenaline's pumping through my veins.

"Have you done your pre-checks?"

"Of course I have," she snaps.

Clearly I am not going to be useful here. I climb down from the booth and go to help the volunteer in the box office. It turns out to be Zach's aunt, Melissa.

"Oh, Zadie! Thank goodness you're here! Do you know where the extra calculator is? This one seems to be out of batteries!"

I decide not to point out she probably has a calculator on her phone. Being in charge of the box office tends to put even the most capable parents into a panic. Melissa is the CEO of a major tech company, but making change for a fifty-dollar bill is freaking her out.

"Here you go." I pull a calculator from the drawer right next to her.

"Oh, Zadie, you're a lifesaver! Actually, can you take over here for a minute?" she asks. "I need to use the bathroom before the show starts."

"Sure!"

I, unlike capable adults, love the box office. There's a lot of power in sitting there and deciding who gets to come in and who doesn't. I mean, anyone who pays gets to come in. But only if I give them their ticket.

The first few people who walk up to the window are longtime BYT parents I've known forever. They're giddy with excitement, mostly, except for the ones who look bored to death, and the show hasn't even started.

Papa and Grandma Sooz arrive together, and Grandma's got a bouquet for Lulu. But it's not flowers. It's lip gloss and nail polish and gel pens with fuzzy tops all bunched together in a colorful bouquet. Way better than flowers, which will only die.

"Cool bouquet," I tell her as I push their tickets through the little hole in the glass.

"For one of my very cool granddaughters," she says with a wink.

After they move on, a group of people who are not the usual BYT patrons steps up. They're way overdressed for children's theater, in dark suits and stiff dresses. They look like they're going to the opera, or a funeral.

"Tickets for Bainbridge Island Council," a bearded man says.

My stomach knots, and I probably turn as green as Mom was this morning.

"Sure." I flip through the will-call tickets, which have already been paid for, until I find a thick envelope with enough tickets for this group. I pretend there's an issue, like I need to count the number of tickets inside and the number of people in their group, but really I'm taking the time to study them.

Jim's not with them; he already came in with Jacob.

The rest of the island council consists of four men and three women, all white. Jim is definitely the youngest. The oldest probably couldn't handle Grandma's Gentle Gyrations class. None of them look like they have the slightest sense of humor.

"Young lady?" the bearded man says. "Our tickets?"

"Sorry." I slide them across. "I hope you enjoy the show. I hear it's really exceptional. And even more importantly, I hear that the children learn social skills, teamwork, and leadership."

He gives me a strange look and takes the envelope.

When Zach's aunt returns, I have just enough time to go to the bathroom myself and climb up to the booth.

The show is about to start!

In the coziness of the booth, I have the best seat in the house, even though I'm farther away from the stage than anyone except Ana María.

She calls the first few cues, and I'm on the light board, listening to her calls, ready when she says, "Lights three, standby." And then I push the little levers up or down a moment later, when she says, "Lights three, go."

The lights flood the stage for the morning scene in the great hall, where Spinderella is having breakfast with her parents, the king and queen, and they are about to tell her she absolutely must be married by her twenty-first birthday or an ancient curse will befall the castle and everyone in it.

Which is why Lulu as Grizelda will disguise herself as a chambermaid and sneak into

Spinderella's room, where she will poison the princess's favorite perfume so that she will fall into a deep sleep and cannot be married in time.

When Spinderella sprays her perfume, there's this important sequence of cues that happen all at once. Onstage, there's a flash pot, which is a cool little device that explodes (safely) with a boom and a flash of smoke. From the booth, Ana María will press the button for a dramatic sound cue that's sort of like thunder. And at the same time, there are three light cues, one right after the other. The normal lights on Spinderella's bedroom come down, while a super-harsh and creepy reddish light comes on, and then, to top it all off, there's a flash like lightning.

Since nothing much is happening for us in the booth during the breakfast scene, my eyes wander up to the lighting grid. I'm thrilled to be in the booth, not lurking but actually doing an important job. But if I could be anywhere else, it would be up on the grid.

If I weren't staring longingly up, I never would have noticed this, but something catches my eye: one of the lights looks super wonky. As in, they're all supposed to be pointed at the stage, at precisely the right angles for what the lighting designer intended. And I wouldn't be able to tell from here if they were a little off. But it also wouldn't be the end of the world. (Maybe it would even put Bladdie in darkness when they're supposed to be in light, ha!)

But this one light I'm noticing isn't only off by a little. It is swung completely around so that it's not even pointing at the stage. It's pointing at the audience, more like.

Maybe it's not an important light. Maybe it doesn't even get used. But that seems unlikely, since Mom's always complaining that she doesn't have enough lights to do what she wants. Probably every light up there gets used.

Still, Ana María would have noticed when she did her pre-checks, right? Pre-checks include running through all the lights to make sure everything's working the way it should. In case a light has burned out or something.

I peek at her, and she's on her phone. Of course. Except not of course! No matter how distracted she is, we're in the middle of a show! Even if it's kind of a boring scene.

"Ana María?" I whisper. I don't really have to whisper; the booth is pretty soundproof, but I'm a little afraid of getting snapped at.

With good reason.

"What?" she snaps. "The show's going on, Zadie."

My point exactly!

"There's a wonky light."

She's still annoyed, but I've gotten her attention away from her phone.

"What are you talking about?"

"That light on the far-right side of the grid. Do you see it? Doesn't it look like it's pretty . . . wonky?"

A few weeks ago, she would have kicked me out of the booth for bugging her. But I'm her ASM now. A fellow woman in tech—at least as long as I'm on this planet. Even in the darkness of the booth, I see her face drain of color.

"It's facing the audience," she whispers.

"That's what I thought." It's unnerving how panicked she looks. I thought telling her was the right thing to do, but now I'm not sure. "Can we just . . . not use that light? So it doesn't turn on and shine into their faces? Is that possible?"

"No, I'd have to rebuild the cues, plus . . ."

She looks more carefully. She's figuring something out. At the same time, I'm looking from the wonky light to the spot in the audience where it's pointing.

"Oh space junk," we both say at the same time.

"It's the creepy red light," she says.

"And it's pointing right at the island council."

20
The Show Must Go On

Even in the midst of this disaster, Ana María takes a second to glance at her phone and grimaces.

"Is everything okay?" I ask.

"No," she says. "Nothing is okay."

"Um . . . okay." At least we're on the same page. My mind races. Ana María seems too distracted by her phone to come up with solutions. I could text my mom, but she'll have her phone off. First rule of Attending the Theater. Papa and Grandma won't have theirs on either; they know Mom's lectures by heart.

Then it comes to me.

"I could climb out on the grid," I say. "And

adjust the light. It wouldn't be perfect, but I could at least point it away from the audience." The island council. I don't know if Ana María even knows about that added complication. She's got too much going on, so I'm keeping quiet about that.

"No way," she says. "Marinee would kill me."

"She wouldn't have to know. We've got . . . what, five minutes until that cue? We have to decide now, but I could do it."

She thinks about it. Oh my shooting stars, she actually thinks about it!

"No," she says finally. "Someone has to do it, but it's not going to be you. I'm going. Which means you're running the board. The book's right there. You know how to do it, right?"

During tech, she let me call some scenes, for practice, using her giant binder with the cues written in the margins of the script.

"I know how to do it."

Without another word, Ana María disappears, and I am left at the controls of a spaceship hurtling into the path of an asteroid.

Sort of. It's really more like a spaceship that's

been well programmed, and I need to do my best with extremely minimal astronaut training.

An awful lot of people are relying on me to be successful, and they don't even know it. Ana María has trusted me—me, the walking disaster!—to steer this ship during an emergency. It's exactly what I've always wanted, even if it's a very different ship than I expected to be commanding. And even if Ana María and I are the only ones who ever know, I need to prove that I can do this.

If I can do this, there really is no limit.

I'm super tense as I do the first few cues. But all goes smoothly, and I get into the groove. All the cues are clearly written out in Ana María's notebook. As long as I pay attention to which button or lever to push and when, I'll be fine. The actors on the stage will never know their fate was in my hands.

I'm distracted for a second by a buzz from Ana María's phone. I'm a little surprised she left it, but thank all the stars in the galaxy. If she'd taken it, it might have fallen out of her pocket while she was up on the grid, and with our luck, it would bonk a member of the island council on the head.

I can't help but glance at the screen and see that it's a call coming in from Abuelo.

Grandpa.

But I have some cues to handle, and even Ana María wouldn't answer a call during the show. She can call him back during intermission.

Only because I'm looking for it, I can make out her shadowy form as she creeps along the grid, above the heads of the audience. Now it makes sense that stage managers dress entirely in black. I glance sheepishly down at my bright purple NASA shirt with rainbow rockets and planets all over it. If she'd let me go out on the grid, someone totally could have spotted me.

The phone buzzes again. A call from Abuelo. Why didn't he just text, or leave a message?

The complicated cue with the flash pot and the red light is getting uncomfortably close. Lulu is already in place as Grizelda, holding the perfume bottle, about to add the potion—

Ana María moves the light into place—or as close as she can guess—right in time, and I call the cues. The flash of powder happens onstage, the sound cue rumbles, the lights bathe the stage in creepy red.

The audience murmurs. I try to see if the island council looks impressed, but it's hard to tell from the backs of their heads.

Another call comes in on Ana María's phone.

By the time she's back in the booth, intermission is starting.

"You did it," we both say when we see each other, and she gives me a double high five.

"I'm not sure I positioned it right," Ana María says.

"It wasn't blinding anyone, so I think that's a win."

"And YOU! You did amazing, Zadie!"

She's weirdly energetic, like she got a big rush out of being up on the grid. Which I totally understand. But I'm not even jealous that she got to go instead of me, because sitting here in the booth, alone at the controls, was pretty much the coolest.

Her phone buzzes again, and her face instantly changes as she grabs for it.

"¿Alo, Abuelo? ¿Estás bien?"

And then Mom pops her head in. "How're my girls?"

Ana María turns to face the corner, talking in hushed whispers. Mom frowns.

"Great!" Mom has enough to worry about, with the island council here and all. She doesn't need to know about the near-catastrophe with the red light. "So great!"

Mom nods toward Ana María. "She hasn't been on her phone during the show, right?" she whispers.

"Her phone? Ana María? What? No way!"

Mom's not buying it.

"Seriously, Mom, did you see any mistakes from the booth in the first act? I don't think so! We're doing great. You go schmooze with the people! We'll talk to you later!"

Mom nods and gives Ana María a little wave that she doesn't see.

As soon as Mom's gone, I head backstage to handle the set changes that need to happen before the second act. I'm tempted to pop into the green room and check on Lulu and Zach. But

I'm worried about Ana María, so I head straight back to the booth as soon as I can.

I find her packing her bag. "Zadie," she says. "I have to go."

"What?"

"I don't have time," she says. "I'm so sorry, but you can handle it. I know you can. It's my abuelo. He fell. My aunt was supposed to be with him, but she's not taking this seriously and she went on the ferry into Seattle."

She's sobbing now. I knew she was going through a lot, but I was unprepared for this—the most in-control person I've ever met, falling apart in front of me.

"I called for an ambulance," she says through her tears, "but he doesn't speak English as well as he understands it, so I'm afraid he won't be able to communicate with them—"

"I've got this." I move out of her way.

It's her abuelo, and he needs help. Of course she has to go. If my grandma needed me, nothing would stop me from getting to her.

Part of me wants to hug Ana María, but I'm pretty sure she's not a hugger, so I just try for a supportive smile, and she's gone.

I check the time. We're supposed to start the second act in two minutes. I peer down at the house. There's Mom, standing with the group from the island council, who all look stiff and formal, and not at all like they've spent the last hour being delighted by the wonders of arts education.

I could go down and get her, have her come up to the booth and run things. Right when I'm pondering that, she glances up. She can't see me; from the outside the booth is dark glass. But I can tell from her stiff smile and tight shoulders that she's hoping the house lights will go to half soon, so she has an excuse to stop talking to the council. That's her only escape, unless I run down and alert everyone to the current disaster.

I hit the button to send the house lights to half. That's the cue for all the people who are still milling around to take their seats. Mom says some last thing to the island council, then heads for her own seat, sending a thumbs-up toward the booth. Where she thinks her totally overqualified stage manager is about to run the show.

But Ana María ran a show for the first time once too. Sure, she probably had a lot more training and someone else in the booth with her. But sometimes there's no chance to prepare. For all the training astronauts do, there's no simulator realistic enough to prepare them for an actual rocket launch. Valentina Tereshkova never got to practice her maneuvers in the Vostok 6 before she was actually in orbit. Alone.

She took the training she had and combined it with her instincts and her courage, and she just did it. I grew up in this theater. It might not have been my dream to do tech, but it turns out it has more than a little in common with my dreams of space flight. Not just the STEM stuff, but the imagination, the courage, the reliance on so many different people with different skills coming together with a mission to explore a new world.

And maybe this universe is big enough to hold more than one kind of dream.

I take a slow, deep breath, and then bring the house lights all the way down.

21
Speak Clearly

By the time I hit the final cue, bringing the house lights back up after the curtain call, I feel like I've run a marathon. No, I've won a gold medal. No, I've orbited the earth forty-eight times on a solo flight.

I'm pumped, is what I'm saying. It went perfectly. At least, as far as I could control it. My timing might not have been as smooth as Ana María's on some of the more complicated sequences, but I don't think anyone noticed. The actors made some mistakes, of course, but mostly it went great. The audience laughed a lot and gave them a standing ovation at the end. (Though to be honest, Bainbridge Youth Theater usually gets standing ovations, because if your parents won't give you one, who will?)

But not everyone out there was a cast member's parent. I peer down at the audience as they stand and greet the people around them and pull bouquets out from under their seats to give to their kids.

The island council stands around chatting with one another. From my angle, it's hard to say, but it seems like they're relaxed and happy. They're not running out the door in horror, anyway.

Was it enough to keep the theater's funding and my mom's job? I don't know. But I do know we couldn't have done any better than we did. So if it wasn't enough, then we'll have to figure that out.

Like Grandma Sooz moving to Florida.

Maybe she'll fly home every time Lulu's in a show. Maybe she'll fly home every time I stage-manage a show! After today, that seems like a possibility.

My duties aren't actually over yet, but I'm way

too pumped to go sweep the stage and put props back into place for tomorrow's performance. I'll get to that stuff, but I'm taking my time walking through the house and greeting people first.

"Hi, Melissa," I say to Zach's aunt. She's beaming as she talks to Mrs. Freymiller. "Zach did great!"

"He sure did," she says. "And so did you!"

I freeze, wondering if she somehow knows I ran the whole second act. "Zadie's been a big help to all the designers," Mrs. Freymiller says, very kindly not mentioning all the ways I made her life harder.

"The costumes were marvelous," Melissa says, and I slip away, eager to get closer to the island council.

"Zig-Zag!" Grandma Sooz appears with what I think is her bouquet for Lulu. Then I notice this one isn't filled with lip gloss and hair ties. It's a bouquet of cookies—outer space–themed cookies. Rockets and planets and astronaut cookies on sticks, all tied together like a bouquet of flowers.

"For me? I wasn't in the show."

Grandma scoffs. "Doesn't mean you weren't a big part in making it a success!"

I take the bouquet with a grin. "Thanks, Grandma. You're the best." I can't help but feel sad, though, too. This is probably the only time she'll ever give me a bouquet for my work on a show. It's not realistic to think she'd fly across the country every time someone in this family needs her. It would cost too much. If she had that kind of money, she might as well stay and pay rent to my parents.

"Hey, chin up." She actually reaches out and tips my chin up. "I know you didn't get your own round of applause, but we both know how hard you worked."

"It's not that. I'm just really going to miss you." I swallow hard and hold the bouquet tight. "Thanks for this. I've still got stage management stuff to do."

"Okay, but wait a minute. Can I get a hug?"

Grandma pulls me tight, and right before she lets go, she says, "I think things are going to work out, Z."

Before I can ask what that means, she's turned

away to talk to someone else, and now I see the island council making their way out of the theater. I climb over a few rows of seats so I can slip into the aisle right in front of their group. Then I nonchalantly step out and walk slowly in front of them.

"I thought it was delightful," I hear Jim say. "Really quite impressive, given their budget."

"But wouldn't the children of our community be better served by STEM options? Technology is how our world works now," a woman's voice says.

"Actually"—I turn around before I can talk myself out of it—"not to eavesdrop, but you're kind of loud, and I'm an actual kid. Have you ever heard of STEAM? A lot of people are using that now instead of STEM. Science, technology, engineering, and math are important. I'm going to be an astronaut, so I get it. But the arts are important too. If everything is all technology with no focus on how to communicate and express emotions and make persuasive arguments, we'd all be robots!"

Jim's eyes twinkle, but he doesn't betray the fact that I've built an actual robot in his living room. (I mean, not actual in the sense that it worked. More of an aspirational robot, I guess.)

One man looks offended that I barged in, which, fair, but the rest are beaming at me.

"Were you in the show?" one of them asks, eyeing my bouquet. "I don't recognize you."

I straighten up. "I'm the ASM. Assistant stage manager."

"Oh!" the youngest woman says. "Are kids a part of the technical elements too? I didn't see that in the program."

"Yes!" I say. "I'm kind of a test program!" It's not strictly true, but it's also not *not* true. "And there's tons of technology in the theater. I learned to build all the light cues into a computer program."

They nod, impressed.

Then a pair of heavy hands descends on my shoulder. "Zadie Louise? What are you up to?"

Mom stands behind me, looking slightly panicked.

"Oh, this young lady was telling us about your pilot program in technical theater! It sounds very valuable!"

Mom's smile freezes on her face. "Oh? Yes. I'd love to tell you more about it. Zadie, you need to restore the props, don't you?"

I grin and escape with my cookies. Honestly, this show is going better than I ever dreamed.

22
Work Together

It's not until the theater has cleared out and only a few stragglers are still chatting in the lobby that Mom finds me up in the booth. She frowns at me shutting down Ana María's computer. Little does she know I was touching it for the whole second act! If I hadn't been, there wouldn't have been a show!

"Where's Ana María?" she asks, no doubt thinking there's no way she would have left without her computer.

"Not here." I'm unsure how much to confess. As much as I'd like to be the hero who saved the show, I don't want to get Ana María in trouble.

"But I already swept and restored the stage, and I'm almost finished up in here. We should be set for tomorrow's matinee."

Mom's omission-detector zeroes in on me. "She didn't leave, did she? Without her computer?"

"Um."

"Zadie? What's going on?"

Suddenly I can't hold it in any longer. Which might have something to do with the seven cookies I've eaten since the show ended. Self-control is a lot harder when sugar's coursing through your veins like fuel surging toward rocket boosters.

I sink onto the recliner and tell her everything. The light facing the wrong way. How I called the cues while Ana María fixed it. The calls from her abuelo and how she had to leave, she had no choice, and there was no way to reach Mom without letting the island council know there was a catastrophe in progress.

"So she just left?" Mom sinks down next to me, her face pale. "At intermission?"

"She had to! Her grandfather wasn't going to be able to communicate with the ambulance guys."

Mom nods. "But who ran the second act? I didn't notice a single hiccup. . . ."

Now that she doesn't seem too overly mad at Ana María, I allow myself to puff up a little. "I did it myself. I mean, she left her call book and the computer with all the cues built in. She'd been showing me how to do it all through tech week. It really wasn't that hard."

"It *was* that hard," Mom says. "It was the most complicated show I've ever done. All trying to impress the island council—and you knew about that, too, apparently?"

"I've had a lot of time to sit around and listen."

She shakes her head in wonder and pulls me in for a hug. "You're making me reconsider my thoughts on kids in tech."

I snuggle into her shoulder. I can't remember the last time my mom and I cuddled.

She pulls back a little and looks at me with a twinkle in her eye. "And I may have my reasons to keep offering student tech opportunities. The island council was very impressed by what you said about STEM and STEAM."

"Are you mad?"

"Mad? Zadie, how could I be mad? You completely saved the day. And you might have saved Bainbridge Youth Theater!"

"Mom? Zadie? Where are you guys?"

I stand up from the couch to see Lulu down on the stage, back in her street clothes but her face still made up like Grizelda, with dark-rimmed eyes.

I flash the lights at her. She waves up at us. "Come on! I want to go home!"

Mom stands, looking exhausted. "What are we going to do about tomorrow's show?"

I shrug. "I stage-managed half the show. Pretty sure I can manage the whole thing."

"Even the best stage managers need an assistant."

"Well," I say over my shoulder as I start to climb down, "you can be my assistant if you want."

When we get home, Papa and Grandma Sooz are making celebratory tacos. It smells amazing. While Lulu tells them about my adventures in stage management—I can't believe she's willing to share the spotlight—Mom stands by the door, texting with a tense look on her face.

"All right," Papa says to Lulu. "Why don't you go wash that makeup off your face so I can have dinner with my daughter and not an evil witch?" He turns to me. "And you, Commander Zadie. What a hero! I'm so proud of you. Aren't you proud, Marinee?"

We all turn to Mom, who's still texting.

"Marinee?"

Her head snaps up. "Oh, sorry. Yes, I am truly so proud. Look, Ana María's all alone at the hospital. I'm going to head over there."

"Oh, hon," Grandma Sooz says, abandoning the sizzling meat on the stove and coming over to put her arm around Mom, squeezing her with a giant lobster-claw pot holder on her hand. "You're exhausted. How about I go instead?"

"Thanks, Mom, but she doesn't know you at all."

"I'll go," Papa offers.

I speak before Mom can object. "Ana María really liked Papa at dinner, remember?"

Papa removes his apron. "You take a load off, have something to eat, get some rest. If you want to come relieve me later, you can. Okay?"

He doesn't wait for an answer. By the time he's done getting his things together, Mom has relented.

"Okay," she says. "I sent you the details. Thank you, love."

He gives her a quick kiss, and me too, and then he's gone.

When I get up (late) the next morning, Papa's at the kitchen table, nursing a cup of black coffee.

"Morning, Commander Zadie," he says. "How'd you sleep?"

"Great. Saving the day is exhausting." I pull out a box of cereal. "How's Ana María? How's her grandpa?"

"She's okay. I was with her until her abuelo came through his surgery and wasn't going to wake up for hours. Ana María was dozing off, so I came home. Mom went early this morning."

"Is he going to die?"

"Die? No. I mean, not yet anyway. He fell

because of some balance issues and broke his hip and collarbone. He's going to need some serious care for a while. Probably the rest of his life."

"It's a good thing Ana María's here, then. So he has someone."

"It is good," Papa says slowly. "But it's not going to be enough. She can't do it herself. That's one of the things we talked about while we were waiting for him to come out of surgery. It's gotten to the point where he's really going to need to go into a facility where there are doctors and nurses available all the time."

Oh. That sounds terrible. Papa has talked before about how strange it is that in the United States it's so normal for old people to move into assisted-living places. In Guatemala it's the most normal thing for grown kids to take care of their parents when they reach that stage of life. Papa was the one who insisted Grandma Sooz move into the basement when her husband died. Not that Grandma needs much taking care of.

She takes care of us. At least for now.

"Aren't those places awful, though?"

Papa frowns into his coffee. "I think that when it's possible, it's good to be with family. But it's not always possible. Ana María's done all she can. She needs some help. It's important to recognize that."

Over the next few weeks, Ana María has a lot of help. Once *Spinderella*'s closed, Mom suddenly has tons of time. She's not diving into preparations for the fall show until we get word on the island council's funding decision. She spends most of that time at the hospital with Ana María, or helping her look at assisted-living facilities.

Sometimes Lulu or I tag along. Which is how I end up sitting on a bench in a gazebo next to Ana María's abuelo, Don Oscar, in his wheelchair. Mom and Ana María have gone inside to tour the facility, but he didn't want to.

I don't blame him. A lot of these places are pretty sad. The people who work in them are all really nice and they're trying to make these old people comfortable, but there's still this grim feeling that when you check into a place like this, you're never checking out.

"Mira el colibrí," he says, pointing out a hummingbird at a nearby sage bush.

We both understand more than we can speak

of the other's language, so we're kind of a perfect pair. I don't know the word he used, but I do at least know the word for bird. "¿Pájaro?"

He nods. "Sí, un colibrí."

I listen carefully this time, then repeat after him. "Un colibrí."

He nods, satisfied that I've learned a new word, and we sit in silence until my mom and his granddaughter come back.

"How was Bainbridge Manor?" Grandma Sooz asks at dinner that night.

"Really great," Mom says. "I think it's the one, though Ana María has to convince Don Oscar to go inside next time. It's really his decision. But it was welcoming, and the staff was very knowledgeable. The rooms were lovely, much more like studio apartments than hospital rooms."

"Is that what the place in Florida is like, Grandma?"

We all turn to stare at Lulu.

"What?" She clatters her fork onto her plate. "Are we just not talking about the fact that Grandma sold Zoom Zoom Zumba and is apparently moving across the country, even though she's never actually said it out loud?"

I'm not always thrilled when Lulu's almost-teenager busts out, but I like this side of her. "Lulu's right." I clatter my fork onto my plate in solidarity. "If you're leaving us for an old folks' home, we deserve to know."

Grandma sets her fork down with much more dignity. "Well, the truth is, I am. But it's not in Florida."

Neither Mom nor Papa looks shocked, which means this is yet another Conversation the grown-ups had without us, as though we didn't deserve to know.

"What, then?" Lulu's eyes blaze. "Hawaii? Vermont? London?"

Grandma waits until Lulu's through listing far-off places. Then she says quietly, "Bainbridge."

Mom and Papa are both smiling, but I don't know what to think. Grandma in an old folks' home doesn't make sense. I know this after visiting them with Ana María this last week. Grandma Sooz is nothing like Don Oscar. She's still independent and healthy! She doesn't need nurses bringing her pills and Jell-O.

"Bainbridge Manor, in fact," she goes on. "But not the assisted-living facility, where Don Oscar will be. I'll be in the retirement home, which is more like an apartment building for active seniors."

"But why?" Lulu says. "You must have to pay rent. So you might as well stay here."

"Lulu," Papa warns.

"It's all right, Felipe. I haven't kept the girls up to date on all of this because it's been constantly changing, and I didn't want to upset anyone until I knew how it was all going to turn out. Ideally, I wouldn't upset anyone at all, but that's life.

"I won't, in fact, have to pay rent at Bainbridge Manor. I'll be doing the same thing my friend in Florida proposed—running the activities program there, in exchange for free rent."

My mind swirls, adjusting to this new information. Grandma Sooz is still moving out. Space junk. But she'll be on Bainbridge? Shooting stars! "So you'll still teach Zumba?"

"Absolutely. And other activities too—bingo

nights and talent shows and trivia bowls. It's a pretty big job—I imagine I could use some assistants from time to time, if anyone was willing."

I'd rather Grandma Sooz stay with us forever, but if she has to move out, this sounds pretty great. Bainbridge Manor is only a ten-minute drive. I might even convince Mom and Papa to let me bike there on my own.

Lulu remains skeptical. Now she turns on Mom and Papa. "So now a stranger will move into our house and pay rent?"

They exchange a Look. "We're working on it," Mom finally says. "Who wants dessert?"

The next weekend, Papa rents a U-Haul to help Grandma Sooz move into Bainbridge Manor. I don't get why they need a whole truck. It's the smallest one, but still. Grandma's moving into a furnished apartment and leaving our basement furnished for the future renter. We could have piled her stuff into our regular car and done it in a couple of trips.

But once her stuff is moved in, we take the truck over to Don Oscar's apartment and help

Ana María move him into Bainbridge Manor. He's also moving into a furnished room and doesn't need much stuff, but we use the truck to help Ana María put some things into storage and take the rest to Goodwill, until the apartment they lived in is empty.

I'm exhausted from hauling stuff in and out of the truck and up and down stairs. But I'm trying to enjoy the time with Ana María. I haven't wanted to ask where she's going. I'm afraid the answer is back to Ashland. Close enough to visit Don Oscar frequently, but a place where she can do professional theater.

But Papa's been teasing a surprise at the end of the day, so I'm trying to focus on that. My money's on a trip to Mora for a giant waffle cone full of blackberry ice cream. (Not that I have any money left over, after dumping it all into candy inventory.)

"That's the last of it," Papa says as we unload an orange flowered couch at Goodwill. "How about we head home?"

Or . . . out for ice cream?

Ana María agrees and climbs into the truck.

I sit between the two of them, expecting at any moment that Papa will take the turn toward the town center and the ice cream shop. But he passes right by it. I sit there while Ana María and Papa chatter back and forth in Spanish. I listen, practicing a few new words after the last couple of weeks around Don Oscar.

Papa pulls into our driveway with a grin. "All righty. One more round of unloading and then I've got to return this truck. Remember that surprise?"

He climbs out, and so does Ana María. What unloading is left?

I scramble out and around to the back, where I see a pile of boxes and bags. Among them, an Oregon Shakespeare Festival tote bag. I stare at Ana María and she grins.

"What? Are you just going to stand there, or are you going to help, roomie?"

She picks up a box and heads toward the back entrance into the basement apartment.

Epilogue

"Hurry up, Zadie," Ana María calls. "I don't want to be late!"

I roll my eyes but grab my bike helmet and hurry outside. Mom and Papa won't let me bike to Bainbridge Manor on my own (yet), but they're happy for me to go with Ana María. And we go almost every day.

Most days I hang out with Grandma Sooz, and Ana María hangs out with her abuelo. Occasionally Grandma and I head over to the assisted-living facility, and we all have lunch with Don Oscar in his room.

Today, though, Ana María is going to take Grandma Sooz's Zumba class while I hang out with Don Oscar. She's thinking of getting certified to teach Zumba herself, because even though the island council approved funding for Mom's full-time salary, there was only enough in the budget for a half-time production stage manager position.

Mom and Papa are keeping her rent cheap, but she's still got student loans and health insurance and blah blah adult money stuff blah. So she's also coaching a junior roller derby team, and I'm her star blocker. (I mean, we've only had the first orientation session, but I'm pretty sure that's how it's going to work out.)

Once Don Oscar and I are settled in the gazebo where he first taught me the word "colibrí," Ana María runs off to sweat with the oldies. I pull out a comic book and sit where he can see as I turn the pages. I've offered to read aloud, but he says he just likes to look.

"¿Cómo está tu hermana?" he asks after a while.

"She's fine. Practicing her audition for the fall show. Super annoying."

A smile dances over his lips. "Cómo friega."

"Cómo friega," I repeat. Don Oscar teaches me the most important words.

"¿Y tu padre?"

"Papa's doing pretty good, actually. He's still driving for Ryde, but he also got a couple of new music students from talking to people who rode with him!"

Don Oscar frowns. I'm not sure he got all that. So I try again, peppering in some Spanish words when I know them. The new music students meant we were able to afford the special skates and helmet and pads I need for roller derby, so I'm good. I'm also going to assistant stage-manage the fall show, *Charlotte's Web*. I'm proud of Lulu for overcoming her fear of giant bugs to audition.

It's kind of ironic how I secretly saved Lulu from a potion bottle full of spiders and now she might even get to play one. Also, I know spiders aren't bugs, but trust me when I say Lulu's fears are not rational. (I'm not judging, as someone who'd rather wrestle a giant spider than stand in a spotlight.)

If Lulu is willing to share the stage with a

giant spider—or potentially even *be* a giant spider—maybe there's a chance that one day I'll face my fears and trod the boards.

But I don't think so. Because for me, it's not really about fear. It's about knowing that I fit somewhere else. Up above the stage, pushing the buttons and pulling the levers that make it all happen.

(Or sometimes, creeping across the grid in the dark. But don't tell.)

Acknowledgments

Writing a book has more than a few things in common with putting on a play. Most of all, they're both collaborations, requiring the talents of many dedicated people. And I had an excellent team working with me on *Zadie*!

Many thanks to my intrepid stage manager (or rather, literary agent) Jim McCarthy, who, like Ana María, somehow knows everything about everything and keeps me on track. Thanks also to the rest of the team at Dystel, Goderich & Bourret.

This production would not exist without a fantastic director at the helm: my editor at Atheneum Books for Young Readers, Reka Simonsen, who was supported by a great crew of stagehands, including her assistant, Kristie Choi; managing editors Jeannie Ng and Kaitlyn San Miguel; and a fantastic publicity and marketing team.

This metaphor is a bit stretched, but the place where it really works is art director Greg Stadnyk as my costume/set/lighting designer on this production! Our cover illustrator, Teresa Martinez, brought Zadie and the Bainbridge Youth Theater to life more perfectly than I could have dreamed.

There's a lesser-known role in the theater called a dramaturg, and they help the playwright with research! I had many dramaturgs on this book, including Jacob A. Climer, Dani Norberg, Amy Poisson, Rebecca Balcárcel, Ismee Williams, Jennifer Jones Vincent, Jennifer Longo, and Cordelia Longo. These wonderful people answered all my questions about technical theater, bicultural families, fostering/adoptive families, and Bainbridge Island. (Any mistakes are mine!) And special shout-out to awesome Seattle-area actor, director, and Chicana activist Ana María Campoy, for the use of her name!

Everyone involved in the theater survives only with the support of family who understand the ups and downs, the long hours, the unique frustrations. My family does double duty, supporting me in my life as a playwright *and* as an author! My wonderful husband, Mariño, keeps us all grounded (no climbing on the grid!), and my children, Cordelia and Joaquin, are the first to leap to their feet for a standing ovation every time I show them something I write.

Finally, you with this book in your hands: you have the starring role of reader! We couldn't put on this play without you!